JESSIE'S SONG

JESSIE'S
SONG

Inspired by a True Story

JEREMY WILLIAMSON

LOST AND FOUND PUBLISHING

For bulk orders or to contact the author, visit:
jessiessong.com

ISBN: 978-0-9992805-0-8 (Print)
978-0-9992805-1-5 (eBook)

Printed in the United States of America
First Printing, 2017
Scripture taken from *The Message*.
Copyright © 1993, 1994, 1995, 1996, 2000, 2001, 2002.
Used by permission of NavPress Publishing Group.

Lost and Found Publishing
Fort Collins, Colorado

For the One in Four

—Isaiah 61

FOREWORD

I'VE MET JESSIE. In fact, I've met Jessie a thousand times with a thousand different faces, and one of the Jessies I've met lives within me. She can be found in all of us, because all of us have stories from our lives we know need to be told. But we have become convinced they are either too much or too little or disqualify us from some experience of belonging we deeply long for but never seem to find.

You too know Jessie. You know her in your friends, in your neighbors, in your coworkers, and especially in your family. But the Jessie you most need to know is the one who calls from deep within you. She has stories you need to hear. More importantly, she has stories you need to tell. Because it is in the telling of your stories—the ones that hold the most fear or shame—that your true heart is set free and you discover who you were truly meant to be *before* the story even began.

Daniel Taylor writes:

> We live in stories the way fish live in water, breathing them in and out, buoyed up by them, taking from them our sustenance, but rarely conscious of this element in which we exist. We are born into stories... Stories make it possible for us to be human. Stories tell me not only who I am but also who you are, and what we are together. In fact, without you and your story I cannot know myself and my story.[1]

As a story-focused trauma therapist, I am continually amazed at the resilience of the human heart. Tragedy permeates our world and deeply affects how we experience and interpret it. And yet, somehow, despite the pain, confusion, and wounding, something rises up in the hearts of valiant men and women who continue to hold onto the hope that *this* is not how it's supposed to be. Somewhere in the recesses of memory, we *know*. Despite how deeply we've been distanced, hurt, rejected, abused, dehumanized, or abandoned, it only takes one ray of hope to rekindle the imagination that we were created for something more.

The Jessie who lives in me says: "But you had a good childhood. What are you complaining about? Other

---

1   Daniel Taylor, *The Healing Power of Stories* (Memphis: Doubleday, 1996), 5.

people had it far, far worse than you." While it may be true that tragedy has a million faces with a million varying degrees of intensity, the fact is that tragedy is still tragedy, and to live in this world is to know it well. No one remains unscathed, and everyone knows the experience of harm in some way. To deny it is to claim deity.

The beauty of a story is in its telling, and through the telling of our stories of harm we find the ability to re-story them in ways we never thought possible. When we acknowledge our stories and bring them into the open and into relationship with trusted people, we realize how blindly we've been living them and how we've traded our glory for a lie.

You were never meant to live under the shadow of tragedy. I am so excited that you have picked up *Jessie's Song*. The fact that you hold this book in your hands means you have joined the rising tide of brave women and men who remember a future you were always meant to live. Through the masterful art of story, Jeremy has written her narrative in such a way that we can all say, "Me too."

As you walk these pages with Jessie, it is my hope that you discover the Jessie who lives in you––the one who faced untold harm, and especially the one who remembers that your story was meant to be epic.

—Chris Bruno, LPC, Author, *Man Maker Project*: *Boys are Born, Men are Made,* CEO, Restoration Project

So if the Son sets you free,
you are free through and through.

—John 8:36

May your journey to freedom now begin.

PROLOGUE

→— · —←

THERE IS ALWAYS a storm brewing in Woodcrest, Texas.

My childhood in that town was like a long, thick-aired day in August. Every sweaty summer morning, the nasty rooster known as Jim Beam jolted me from sleep with a crow that started off strong, wilted two-thirds of the way in, and ended in a whimper. I hated that sound, but I respected it. It meant Mom was in the kitchen making biscuits, and I had ten minutes to get in and out of the henhouse before Daddy was up asking for his eggs.

By nine o'clock, the early stillness would give way to a light breeze. It was the perfect time to feed the hens and clean up the privy before the sun turned the swampland into a sauna. Four hours later, with my chores done, I'd lay my back on the thick St. Augustine grass, flick fire ants off my legs, and watch massive cloud pillars float across the sky and stack themselves all the way to heaven.

Around five each evening, a hot wind would kick up and blow dust in my eyes as the spooky sky tinged our world in yellow. As though on cue, the hair on my arms would stand up, and Jim Beam would cower under the rusty porch chair. That's when my brother Jake would relieve Rowdy, our stallion, of his saddle and lead him back to the barn for the night. Trixie, the German Shepherd we adopted from our cousins, would either follow them to the barn or follow me into the house.

Everyone and everything was prepared, because every night brought a storm—a violent, loud, and terrible storm. Nights were terrifying for us Jenkins kids, because long after the thunder quit and the rain rolled out, another kind of tempest would rage *inside* our four walls.

Mom's childhood had not prepared her for this kind of life. She grew up in a happy, hardworking family with a large chicken farm near Mena, Arkansas. Her dad saved a portion of the farm's earnings each year for family trips to the far corners of America and beyond. They were unlikely globetrotters, but they saw it all—even the changing of the fuzzy-hatted guards at Buckingham Palace.

Mom and Daddy first met in Houston during late summer when Mom was moving into the dorms at Wesley Methodist University. There are few pictures of her from those days but, in all of them, she is striking. Her thick black hair reached just past her shoulders, and she wound some of it into a small beehive on top. Her warm brown eyes seemed to invite others into her open heart. She was a good girl who served her good God. Her simple hope was to find a good man and do good things with their life together.

When they met, Daddy's plan was to spend a week in Houston trying out for various jobs with the oil companies. He had just returned from his second tour of duty in Vietnam. His first tour, with an infantry division deep in the jungle, ended badly, with either bullets or malaria taking most of his friends. After that, he was assigned to work maintenance on big Zippo Flamethrower tanks. It gave him a break from combat and raised his hopes of working on a rig or at a refinery in the booming Texas oil industry.

The story, I'm told, started when Mom went picnicking with some girl friends in a park downtown. Daddy spotted them and overthrew a baseball in their direction so he could retrieve it and meet the pretty girls on the blanket. Mom's friends didn't buy the ruse. They turned away just enough to let Daddy know they weren't interested. Good Methodist girls didn't talk to shirtless strangers, and certainly not wartime strangers with buzz cuts. Mom wasn't any less a Methodist than they, but something about the look on Daddy's face drew her in. She saw questions in his hazel eyes that she wanted to answer and pain that she hoped to help heal.

Daddy seemed to have it made. His skills landed him a job, and his hazel eyes won him a bride. At the family farm on a spring day in 1972, he and Mom stood before a Methodist minister and became Mr. and Mrs. Robert Jenkins.

It was an imperfect union. Grandpa never cared for Daddy. Having employed ex-convicts and other men of questionable standing for many years, Grandpa had a nose for the good and bad in people. Mom knew about his misgivings but was charmed by Daddy and by her secret quest to find the hurting boy behind his strong arms and soft eyes.

She was right. There *was* a boy inside the man with the buzz cut. But he was buried far deeper in the dark part of Daddy's heart than she realized. When the downturn came to the oil industry, Daddy's drinking spiked. His soft eyes seemed to harden and his strong arms delivered more pain than Mom could ever heal, no matter how good a girl she was.

CHAPTER 1

$\rightarrowtail\cdot\leftarrowtail$

THERE WERE SIX of us Jenkins kids. Among the three girls—Katherine, Daisy, and me—Katherine and Daisy were far more interested in wearing Mom's high heels and having tea parties with Grandma's fancy cups than I was. While they dolled up in ruby lipstick, I embarked on endless adventures in the woods with my brother Jake. He was the oldest and strongest of the siblings, but I was faster and could throw a rock almost twice as far as he could.

I wasn't as close with my other brothers as I was with Jake, but I loved them all the same. Jason was the middle boy and Ben—precious little Ben—was barely two and still in diapers. Jason was born with health issues no one ever discussed. The only thing we kids knew was that he went to the doctor a lot, and Mom regularly reminded us that his name means "healer." I suppose that comforted

Mom and maybe even helped Jason, who was at least well enough to attend school.

At each day's end I was like any other little girl who has a daddy. My heart leapt as a cloud of dust arose at the far end of our driveway, and Daddy's powder blue Chevy pickup with the dark blue topper emerged. I loved the hugs and smiles he usually brought home. At the beginning of the month, his grin was euphoric. It was payday, and Daddy always arrived with a bottle of whiskey, a half-case of Lone Star beer, and, sometimes, six root beer suckers for us kids. Soon, however, his euphoria would fade. When money was short again, all Daddy could muster after a hard day's work was a scowl and a little Lone Star.

Those were usually the nights when another kind of storm rolled in. One of the worst ever to hit the Jenkins family came in mid-May, when school was about to dismiss for the summer break. It was Sunday, and Daddy had weekend duty at the refinery. Following his orders, Jake and I worked on the hole for the new fruit cellar. We dug all day, pausing only to rub down our callouses, eat lunch, and chase Rowdy from sticking his head through the kitchen window and into Mom's fruit basket.

When Jake quit digging, I decided to keep going until Daddy came home. I could tell by the position of the sun and the scent of dinner cooking that he was running late. I kept imagining his arrival: He'd catch me working hard, pull me up out of the hole with his thick arms, and hug me tight. Over dinner, he would gush about the fine hole Jake and I had dug and about the new cellar he was going to make of it. He would turn and smile at me. My heart would leap and I would smile back.

My imagination shut down when Daddy's absence became too strange to ignore. I stopped digging, climbed out of the hole, hung my shovel in the shed, and went inside the house, where a peculiar quiet had set in.

Sprawled out on the living room carpet, Jake nervously stacked Legos. Perched in the front window with Trixie, Daisy awaited the dust cloud and the light blue truck. Katherine quietly set the table, careful not to clank the plates. I cracked my knuckles and entered the kitchen, where the look on Mom's face and her intensity in mashing the potatoes confirmed my sense that something was not right.

Unease was not unusual in our house. Unpredictability was. Each day ran like clockwork: I checked off my chores, ate a quick breakfast, and either raced to the end of the driveway to catch the school bus or into the woods to chase a new adventure. Every day ended at roughly the same time, with the sound of Daddy pulling up the driveway and shutting off his engine.

That routine broke down on this day.

Finally, Daisy squealed, "It's Daddy!" and the peculiar quiet was over.

I watched Daddy lumber through the door carrying his keys, jacket, and a half-case of beer. His ruddy cheeks and faraway look told me he was already drunk.

We dutifully continued the evening rituals, as though pretending that everything was all right would make it so. Daisy wrapped her arms around Daddy's leg as he marched through the living room. Trixie wagged her tail and followed close behind. Jake uttered a greeting, but stopped mid-sentence, realizing he was being ignored.

Without a word, Daddy pressed past us, lurched down the hallway, and shut himself into the master bedroom.

We stood almost motionless, gazing at the closed door and wondering what was next. We tried to read the sounds—the flushing toilet, the strange thuds and scraping noises—but we could not. So Mom rushed back to the stove to flip the pork chops.

"Come to the table now," she said. "Supper will be ready in a minute."

Katherine squeezed Ben's chubby legs into the high chair as we all crammed into our places at the table. Sitting elbow to elbow, we waited for Daddy.

Tension filled the atmosphere but, as always, Mom was an absolute wonder. She reminded me of the iconic Lady Liberty standing tall in the harbor that lapped the decayed edges of New York City. Her face was weathered but beautiful, and the coolness in her eyes contradicted her surroundings.

That's my mom, I thought, *a perfectly dignified lady who got stuck living in a dump.*

My back ached from sitting too straight and still for too long. Waiting was even harder for my younger siblings. No one knew where to look, so we focused on the pat of butter melting atop the mound of potatoes. In silence we watched the small yellow mass slide toward the side of the bowl.

"Food's gettin' cold, Mom," said Jake, stating the obvious.

"You just mind yourself," Mom answered sharply. "We'll not touch a morsel until your Daddy's with us and we have said grace." With that, she spread out some green beans on Ben's high chair tray, to keep him from fussing while we waited.

Another excruciating minute passed. There was too much time to think. Clearly, something was wrong. For one thing, Daddy was drunk *before* dinner. He usually got drunk later in the night. The atmosphere in the kitchen was scary, like the previous spring when the afternoon sky turned green, and everyone rushed to their storm cellars. No one knew what would happen next, but everyone knew it would be bad.

CHAPTER 2

THE LONGER WE WAITED, the harder my heart beat. I stared across the table where a single tear traced a path down Jason's cheek.

Then two more thuds broke the silence, and the bedroom door creaked open.

Daddy bounded to the table and sat down. I could tell that he'd showered. His hair was wet and he smelled like Old Spice. A sleeveless undershirt aired splotches on his neck and chest that matched his red cheeks. The shower had curbed but not cured his intoxication. Not that he wanted to be sober; he'd barely sat down before bouncing up again to grab a Lone Star from the fridge.

After he cracked it open, Mom cleared her throat and fixed her eyes on the tablecloth. "Daddy, will you say grace?" Her cheery intonation contradicted the thick atmosphere in which we folded our hands and bowed our heads.

For the first time that night, Daddy spoke, in a simmering, wobbling voice. "Our Lord, we thank thee for the bounty of this table…"

When he stopped mid-prayer, I opened tiny slits in my eyes to see his face contorted as though some dark emotion controlled him. My heart raced as I squeezed my eyes completely shut.

"And, God—Jesus!—I want you to know that I'm about to go down to that refinery an' do something real bad to those greedy liars. I'll probably kill 'em, and I hope you'll forgive me."

"Robert!"

Before Mom's lips closed, Daddy thrust his open hand right up to her face, and shouted, "You shut up while I'm praying to our Lord!"

We shook with dread and kept our hands folded as Daddy aimed the rest of his prayer at the ceiling.

"And I'll kill 'em, Lord," he declared, waving his arms wildly. "I'll kill 'em for not understanding that I have… one…two…three…four…five…six…seven…eight mouths to feed. You know what it takes to clothe these kids and how many doctor bills we have for Jason. That's right, Lord. *You know. And you know this house ain't big enough for this family, neither.*"

Mom figured out what Daddy was getting at. "Robert, you lost your job!"

It was unusual for her to interrupt him, especially in such an accusatory tone. I cringed, anticipating what might happen next.

Then it happened. Seething with rage, Daddy launched the heavy bowl of mashed potatoes straight at Mom's head. She cried out in pain as it drilled her left eyebrow, careened to the floor, and shattered.

In shock, Mom scraped potatoes and blood from her face and hair. Blood ran sickeningly red and fast over the white stuff clinging to her face.

I was also in shock, unable to react. What I saw was too terrible. My beautiful, tireless mom was broken and bleeding because the man I called *Daddy* was a monster. Horrified, I could only tremble.

Jake broke the silence, standing up so forcefully that his chair jerked back and tipped over in a single motion. His eyes were on fire as he thrust his finger dangerously close to Daddy's face and screamed, "You leave my mom alone!"

With a lightning-quick backhand, Daddy smashed Jake's nose. The strike was powerful enough to send Jake crashing to the floor. He lifted himself up slowly, then ran out the side door, holding his face as it gushed all over his hands.

With her dignity intact despite her appearance, Mom said, "Kids, make your plates and take them to your rooms."

I wasn't hungry, but I obeyed.

"Katherine," Mom said, "make a plate for Ben. He can eat with you girls."

In our room, my sisters and I found Trixie quivering beside the bed. I don't know whether she was reacting to the storm in the kitchen or the lightning that flashed outside. To me, the sights and sounds of the outdoor storm seemed comforting compared with what we had just witnessed.

None of us spoke as we set down our plates on the bed or as Katherine went back to the kitchen to get Ben. From the bedroom I heard her shout, "Daddy, you don't have to be so mean! You don't have to hurt Mom like that! I hate you!"

I hoped that Daddy's rage had all been spent. But as Katherine returned with Ben, I realized it wasn't. Her words triggered a second explosion in the kitchen, where Mom begged for mercy while Daddy struck her repeatedly. His thirst for violence seemed insatiable. His vile obscenities and revolting threats knew no end.

Against my better judgment, I peeked into the kitchen to see Daddy yanking Mom by her hair.

I knew none of us could stop him.

Twenty minutes later, the shouting had ended. All of us kids, except for Jake who was still missing, were lined up in the hallway with our hands against the wall and the backs of our legs exposed. We were waiting for the switch. The switch was nothing new, but this night was different.

As we waited to be punished, questions raced through my mind: *Why is Daddy doing this? Did he lose his job on account of me? What did I do to make him so mad?* I wondered whether this would have happened if I had behaved better. I thought, *Maybe if I dug the hole faster, or ate less, or didn't outgrow my shoes so fast, Daddy might not get so drunk. Maybe he wishes I were dead. If only he would stop, I would gladly go without eating and without shoes for all eternity.*

My thoughts were interrupted by the switch slicing through the air, drawing shrieks of pain and sending Katherine sobbing to our room. Jason was next. He tried not to flinch, but a moan leaked out as he fled with his face in his hands. Daisy got it next. She yelped once and walked away in silence. I was next and pleasantly surprised to feel so little pain, although I did seem to have a thousand-pound weight pressing against my chest.

Ben whimpered the whole time, wandering uncomforted in his sagging diaper. He didn't fully understand what was happening, but I could see that he was distressed.

Then Daddy grabbed me with his strong hand and spun me around. "Get Ben," He growled.

"What?"

Daddy just stood there.

"No!" I protested in horror.

"You get him and bring him here!" Daddy commanded as he yanked my face up to his own, his eyes bloodshot and his breath smelling like rotten fruit.

Overwhelmed by his depravity, I turned toward the kitchen. "Mom! He wants to hit Ben!"

Mom was slumped over the kitchen table, either physically or emotionally unable to respond.

I whipped back around and argued with all my strength. "Ben is still a baby! What is wrong with you? He doesn't deserve this!"

Daddy answered in a voice so deep and measured that it terrified me. "Jessie, if you don't get Ben, I will!"

"Fine!" I shrieked. I knew there were no good options, and Ben would probably be more terrified if Daddy handled him.

So I picked up my baby brother and carried him to the wall. He felt so light as I lifted him and set him down. I will never be able to erase the memory of holding his soft, dimpled hands against the wall as Daddy drew back the switch.

Every time Ben cried out, something terrible tore through my heart.

CHAPTER 3

＞—·—＜

WHAT DADDY DID to Ben broke me and left Ben confused and bawling in pain. When it was over, I handed Ben over to Katherine and ran outside and into the darkness as fast as my legs would carry me. I couldn't breathe. I couldn't think. I didn't even feel the rain soaking through my hair and clothing. I had no plan or destination in mind. I wasn't even sure why I was running. I simply kept going for what felt like miles, jumping over brush and ducking under branches.

The thought of stopping never occurred to me until I reached a part of the woods I'd never seen before. There, standing under a tree, I caught my breath and looked around. For the first time, I realized that I was drenched in rain and sweat.

The rain continued falling, but I didn't care. The mostly hidden moon threw just enough light to reveal a massive old log several yards from where I stood. Giant branches stuck out from it, and its bark looked like ten million puzzle pieces glued together. Part of the log was buried in the soil. The exposed part was as long as a school bus. I figured it would take the linked arms of three grownups to encircle it.

I had never seen a tree that big in Woodcrest. Later in life I learned that it was probably a ponderosa pine. Even in the darkness I could tell it was mostly hollow and full of holes, like it had been there for ages, serving as home for any number of creatures.

Holding onto a wobbly branch, I climbed up the log and sat down, the rough bark grating against the welts on my calves. I wondered how Ben's legs looked by now and how Mom and Jake were doing. I replayed the scene in my mind, over and over and over again.

After awhile, my thoughts wandered. For what seemed like an hour, I ran my hand across the tree's bark, picking off the loose puzzle pieces and tossing them to the ground. At some point, the rain let up and the clouds gave way to more moonlight. Instead of the brightness comforting me, it made for an even eerier-looking forest.

Suddenly I felt horribly vulnerable and confused. My lower lip quivered as I thought of my strong, handsome Daddy. I wanted his arms wrapped tightly around me. At the same time, I didn't want him to touch me ever again. I longed to sit on his lap, lean back against his chest, and feel his heart beating as I reached up and rubbed the scratchy whiskers on his chin. I imagined myself saying that I was sorry and that I forgave him for being angry. Then he would smile at me, call me his little Jess, and throw me up on his shoulders.

In the whole world, I wanted nothing more. But somewhere deep inside I didn't want it at all. Either way, I knew I could never have it. To Daddy, Jessie was a disappointment. She was too much work and too expensive to care for. She wasn't smart or pretty enough, and she never worked hard enough to please him. Jessie was always something less than what Daddy expected.

I knew these things but did not understand what made them so. Why wasn't I enough? How hard should I have worked? How smart and pretty did I need to be? I couldn't say. I only knew that something about me made Daddy wish I was someone else—the kind of daughter who made him proud. He would never have a place in his heart for me. I would always be alone—as alone as I was in that moment.

The realization was crushing.

Suddenly I heard branches snapping very close to where I sat. My face went cold with terror. I slid off the log and turned my ankle on a half-buried branch. I was sure I sprained it, but a rush of adrenaline overrode the pain as I moved toward the open end of the log.

The sound of footsteps drew closer. I had to hide, and fast. I couldn't see whether anything was living inside the log, but I didn't care, either. I dropped onto my belly and inched into the opening feet first so the spiders wouldn't feed on my face.

By this time, I was convinced that the nearing footsteps belonged not to an animal but a person. It couldn't be Daisy or Katherine. They would never venture this far. It wasn't Jake or Jason, either. Their footsteps would not be this heavy. I hoped the footsteps weren't Mom's, because I wasn't ready to see her. I certainly didn't want to see Daddy. The thought of being alone in the woods with him was more than I could bear.

Then the sound of crunching leaves and snapping twigs stopped.

Inches from the open end of the log, I saw a man's bare feet and calves bathed in moonlight. The man wasn't Daddy, but I still trembled as he stood there for an overly long moment. It was all too much—too scary, too unknown, too threatening. I wondered, *Will this night of horror never end?*

Ready to explode from fear, I decided to cry for help. But before I could make a sound, the man started humming. His voice was gentle, yet it pierced the air and seemed to stop the world in that moment. I soon realized that he was singing words in a language from an unknown place, somewhere far from Texas.

The melody so captivated me that I stopped trembling and exhaled deeply, releasing all fear from my being and sending it into the darkness. Overwhelming peace replaced the sense of doom, and even my muscles seemed to breathe more easily.

From my hiding place, I watched the man's feet move out of sight as he sat upon the log. He continued to fill my ears with his sweet music. I felt heat radiating from within my chest as though my heart were wrapped in a warm blanket. The experience was inexplicable and begged many questions. *Who was this man? Why did his song affect me so profoundly? Why wasn't I afraid anymore?*

Savoring the moments, I closed my eyes and felt like I was soaring. There was such hope in the man's voice. His words and music rolled through my heart in waves of contentment, security, and love like nothing I'd ever felt before. I couldn't understand his language, but I knew that he was repeating the same few lines over and over again, like a poet does with a chorus.

Somehow I sensed that the stranger was aware of my presence. I felt that he was singing for me and about me, as though we were not strangers at all. I wished his song would never end, and he seemed to grant my wish by singing it for seeming hours. With each refrain, something new and wonderful was revealed, something I could not put into words.

At some point, I realized that the pain in my ankle was gone! *What just happened? I wondered. Is this man some kind of miracle worker?*

Then Jake's unmistakable voice replaced his. "Jessie! Jessie! You there?"

"Jake!" I cried while wiggling out of the log. "How did you find me?"

"I've been looking since you ran from the house. Catching up with you wasn't easy." Jake's voice was in a lower register than normal. He spoke with a calm, manly authority, as though he had grown up that very night.

As I brushed off spider webs and dirt from my front side, Jake got behind me and brushed my back.

"Hey," I said, turning around to face him, "Did you hear—"

I gasped as the moonlight shone on Jake's face. His right eye was swollen nearly shut. The bridge of his nose was two or three times its normal size and moved sharply to the left. Dried blood caked his parched lips and strong chin.

If I'd had the capacity to process everything that happened that night, I would have wrapped my arms around my brother and cried with him. But I didn't. I just stood there with my mouth open, horrified at Daddy's brutality.

In perfect unison, my body and mind decided that it was too much to bear. I threw up, turning my head just quickly enough to avoid adding insult to Jake's injuries. Our shoes did not fare as well.

"Let's go home," Jake said calmly.

It was a long walk back to the house. Nothing would be fixed there, but I was returning with something I did not have before I left—a secret. I decided to keep it to myself, at least for now.

CHAPTER 4

"HURRY UP WITH THOSE EGGS, Jessie! The bus'll be here in five minutes!"

On the morning after the big storm, Mom shouted out the kitchen window like she did every other day. We were running later than usual and had puffier eyes than normal. But at least Daddy was sound asleep and couldn't possibly be mad that his eggs were not collected yet.

I never could understand how Mom managed to feed us and get us out the door each day. On this morning she had even more to do, and with far less sleep. By the time we were up, she had long pants ready for us to wear. They would look odd considering the heat, but sending us to school in shorts would pose a much bigger problem. There was no way to prevent people seeing Jake's busted nose, but no one had to see the red stripes on the Jenkins kids' legs.

I unlatched the screen door to the henhouse and stepped inside, glad to be alone in my smelly little sanctuary. My custom was to peek into the first nest box while humming a song. Then I'd make my normal rounds, spooking away the hens and gathering up their brown and yellow eggs until I reached the third or fourth box.

On this morning, I hummed a new song. It was the first time I'd thought about it or the man in the woods since the night before. I wondered briefly whether the encounter had happened in a dream. But when the man's melody filled my ears again, I knew that I had actually seen him. The tune didn't sound as sweet as when he sang it, but the melody still made me feel safe and warm.

"The bus! The bus! The bus!" Jason's voice snapped me back to reality.

The bus was already at our mailbox. Jason, Katherine, and Daisy sprinted down the drive to meet it while I ran inside to drop off the eggs and grab my backpack. Mom was there, quietly talking to Jake as she straightened his collar. She avoided looking in his eyes as she prepared him for the questions he would face at school.

"You were checking Rowdy's hooves for thrush, and he kicked you square in your face. Got it?"

Jake answered uneasily, "Yes, Mom."

"And if the school nurse wants you to go to the doctor, you tell her we can't afford it right now. Tell her your father will get your nose set back in place once the swelling goes down. OK?"

"OK."

Jake was all cleaned up, but he looked even worse than he did the night before. His eye was completely shut, and the distance between it and his disfigured nose was a multicolored expanse of mostly purple.

The bus horn blared as Mom looked straight into Jake's eyes. Her heartbreak was as plain as the injuries on his face. As though afraid to let him go, she continued to fidget with his already straightened collar.

The horn blared again, making it easier for me to interrupt them. "We gotta go right now, Jake."

Mom flashed me a sweet smile, placed one hand on each of our shoulders, and sent us out the door. Even after years of struggle and violence, Mom's femininity remained intact. Her touch was still as soft as a good feather pillow.

Jake and I ran to the bus together. I couldn't help but race him, even with my long jeans scraping the broken skin on my calves.

Lady Bird Johnson Elementary School was a wonderland to me. I loved my school and loved learning, especially reading and art. With one or two exceptions (the grumpy front-desk clerk, Mrs. Blevins, being one of them), the faculty and other grownups at school seemed to enjoy their work. They knew how tough life was for oil families, so they were kind to us—especially the jolly ladies in the cafeteria who fed us very, very well.

Jake was a grade ahead of me, so we never attended class together. But we met at recess every day to compete in the favorite school game: tetherball. Ashley Liddell was the reigning champion, so my ultimate goal was to dethrone her. I was good at getting the ball going, but my hand-eye coordination tended to undermine my defense. Even so, I never shied away from the game. I figured that either Jake or I would escort Ashley to second place someday.

It would not be on this day.

"Jessie, would you come with me for a minute?" The voice belonged to Jake's teacher, Mrs. Forester. She was the nicest of all the teachers, but something in her voice made my stomach drop.

Without a word, I followed her down the hall to the main office where Jake, Jason, Daisy, and Katherine were already seated in brown and orange folding chairs.

"What's wrong?" I asked, knowing exactly what was wrong.

"Nothing, honey," Mrs. Forester said unemotionally. "Mr. Carter wants to have a quick chat with you and your siblings. Please take a seat, and he'll be right out."

"But it's recess!" protested. "I was going to play—"

"Jessie," a sterner voice added, "this is more important than recess. You can play after school."

It was crabby Mrs. Blevins piping up from her front-desk perch. She always got under my skin, but now she got me good. A smart answer came to mind, but I knew this was not the time to use it. So, I released a dramatic sigh, took the only empty seat, and leaned into my brother.

"You're gonna say it was Rowdy, right Jake?"

"I think so," he whispered.

His answer worried me, but Mr. Carter's arrival allowed me no time to fret.

"Jenkins kids," he said, "please join me in my office. Mrs. Blevins, would you come in as well?"

Without a word, we filed in to Mr. Carter's office. Because there were too many kids and too few seats, my siblings and I stood awkwardly around his desk. Mrs. Blevins stationed herself at the door.

Mr. Carter took his seat and launched the conversation with no introduction. "Jake, I want you to tell me what happened to your face. It looks really bad, buddy."

I assumed that calling Jake *buddy* was Mr. Carter's way of gaining his trust. The tactic was wasted on Jake. Speaking slowly and deliberately, he stuck to the script Mom gave him.

"I was checking my dad's horse...you know...his hooves...for thrush."

"And he kicked you?"

"Yes, sir. He doesn't like anyone lifting up his back hooves. I was hoping he wouldn't give me any trouble, but he got me square in the face."

Mr. Carter's next question caught me off guard.

"Jessie, what about you? Were you with Jake when he got hurt?"

"Uh...yes. I mean...well...no."

I cleared my throat and collected my wits. "I was at home, but I wasn't in the barn."

"What were you doing?"

I wondered why Mr. Carter would care.

"I was out digging in the hole." I realized my answer didn't make much sense, so I continued. "My dad wants to make a fruit cellar for canned stuff from our Grandma's garden."

"So you do all the digging?"

"Well, yes. Me and Jake." My face flushed, and I clenched my teeth to keep from crying.

Mr. Carter exhaled dramatically. "Sandra—er, Mrs. Blevins—I'd like to take a look at the children's legs. Will you help me with that, please?"

Mrs. Blevins reacted with an uncharacteristic hint of emotion. "Yes, of course, Mr. Carter."

My stomach churned as they rolled up our pant legs, one by one. When they finished, Mr. Carter said, "Turn around, children. Let me see the backs of your legs."

I wanted to blurt out some defense, but I knew it would be useless. There was no legitimate excuse for our condition. The best story I could think of—that the stripes were birthmarks genetically dealt to every Jenkins kid—would not hold water, even if it was true at some level.

Except for his pronounced exhalations, Mr. Carter completed his inspection in silence. With a punctuating breath, he said, "Mrs. Blevins, can I see you outside?"

As they squeezed past us and out the door, Mr. Carter said, "You can roll down your pants now. We'll be back in one minute."

Mr. Carter pulled the door shut behind him.

Immediately, Daisy burst into tears. She wasn't the only one. Through the glass pane in the principal's door, I saw Mrs. Blevins dab her eyes with a tissue as she nodded her agreement with whatever Mr. Carter was telling her. The look on her face told me all I needed to know.

"Stop crying, Daisy." Jason, who never said much, was talkative now. "What are they gonna do, Jake?"

Before Jake could answer, Mr. Carter swung the door wide open, and motioned for us to join him in the outer office. "Come," he said, forming us into a huddle. "Remember that I'm your principal, but I'm also your friend. You can trust me."

Like a coach comforting his team after a big loss, Mr. Carter made extended eye contact with each of us.

Seemingly satisfied that he had cemented the bond, he said, "If there is ever anything you want to talk about, even scary or strange things, you can talk to me, OK?"

We looked at Mr. Carter respectfully but gave him little feedback.

He drew us in a little closer. "Listen. I'll give you a special deal that none of the other kids around here get."

Only Daisy smiled.

"Anytime, any day, even during a test, you can tell your teacher that you need to talk to Mr. Carter. Your teacher will excuse you from class, and you can come down and see me. OK? Does that sound good?"

"Yes, sir," replied Jason and Daisy in one voice.

"All right, then," said Mr. Carter. "You can go to recess now."

It was the best thing Mr. Carter could have said, but he quickly changed his mind.

"Hold on kids. Just one second." He poked his head into the nurse's office. "Hey Nancy, do you have any more of those—yeah, those."

Looking back at us, Mr. Carter said, "There are six of you kids altogether, right?"

"Yes sir," I offered. "Ben is the baby. He's at home"

After our ordeal, the idea of a surprise brightened my spirits. Then the nurse placed six cellophane-wrapped toothbrushes in Mr. Carter's hand. My heart sank as each of us chose the color we wanted. Katherine picked one for herself and one for Ben.

"Sorry kids. I don't have any toothpaste," the nurse said in an overly sympathetic way. Then, flashing a massive smile as if to show us what clean teeth should look like, she asked, "Jessie, do you have some at home?"

"Uh huh." I lied.

The truth was that the food bank had stopped giving us toothbrushes and toothpaste, so Mom taught us to mix some baking soda and salt and rub it all over our teeth with our index fingers. Apparently, it had not worked very well, so I refused to heap any more humiliation on my family by mentioning it.

Visiting the principal's office was bad enough. Missing recess was worse. For the remainder of the afternoon, I feared being summoned to the counselor's office or to Mr. Carter's again. The thought of it kept me on edge.

I was pleasantly surprised when the rest of the day turned out normal, except for the fact that most teachers were especially nice to me. In fact, from that day forward it seemed like Mr. Carter went out of his way to smile and say hello each time we passed each other in the hall. Often he would reach into his pocket and produce a brightly colored sucker or Jolly Rancher, offering it to me with a wink and a shushing finger over his lips. I never saw him give suckers away to other kids, not even my siblings, which made me feel good about myself.

Finally, the school day ended. Because the Jenkins house was second to last on the bus route home, I had plenty of time to think. Only in retrospect can I see that my thinking usually centered around Daddy—not my Daddy, but the good daddy I had created in my imagination. We laughed a lot together. We snuggled on the couch and watched old shows. He taught me about things and always had something kind to say. For the next several weeks, the daddy in my imagination looked just like Mr. Carter.

When we reached our stop, I saw that Daddy's truck was not in the driveway. I wasn't particularly thinking about the night before or about Daddy being out of work again, so I was a little surprised to find him sitting at the kitchen table where Mom served us hugs and apple slices after school each day.

"Where's Mom?" I asked, my pulse quickening as my sense of reality returned. I had not spoken to Daddy since the night before, when I begged him not to beat my baby brother.

"She's at Dean's Place," Daddy answered without looking away from his newspaper. "She'll be working there from now on."

"Where's Ben?" asked Katherine.

I assumed that Katherine and I were thinking the same thing. *Surely Mom wouldn't leave Ben alone with Daddy. Not after last night.*

"He's playing in your room."

Katherine pressed the issue. "So, Mom isn't going to be home during the day anymore?"

"No, and maybe not the nighttime either. Not until I can get a better job somewhere."

At least Daddy was sober. But he seemed not to care that we kids would have to manage without Mom.

I knew she was working for our sakes. Mr. Dean was a good friend of the family who owned a diner and truck stop off the interstate. Before Ben was born, Mom had worked for him on and off, cooking and waiting tables. I didn't mind her going back to work. What scared me was the thought of being with Daddy every day. *What if he gets drunk while Mom is working? Who will stand up for us? What if he never goes back to work? What will happen then?*

I was sure Katherine had questions of her own. Knowing how outspoken she could be, I decided to keep the peace by keeping her occupied. "Katherine, come help me dig the pit for the fruit cellar."

Daddy answered for Katherine, "No Jessie. Not today." Looking up from his paper for the first time, he said, "I want Katherine and Daisy to come hunting with me."

"Hunting? Katherine asked.

"When?" added Daisy.

"Tonight," said Daddy. "Go pack what you need."

Jake and I blurted out, "You're taking Katherine and Daisy hunting?"

My sisters were the last people on earth to pick for a hunting trip. They hated dirt. They despised the woods. And they could not keep quiet for five seconds in a row. I knew they would never want to go hunting. And if they did, they'd scare off anything Daddy hoped to shoot.

"Why are you taking *them*?" Jake whined.

"Well, you won't be any help with that eye swol' shut, now will you?" Daddy was already getting angry. "Besides, you and Jessie need to keep digging. Your grandparents will be canning in a few weeks, and that cellar has to be ready."

"But Daisy and Katherine? They don't even like being outside!"

Instead of slapping my hand over Jake's mouth like I wanted to, I pulled him by the collar, all the way outside. "I know how you feel, Jake. I would give anything to hunt with Daddy. But bugging him about it will only make him mad. You know he never changes his mind when he's mad."

Jake shrugged and kicked some pebbles, looking down through his one open eye.

We fetched our shovels in silence and returned to the hole. Jake and I loved hunting and coming home with a kill. If I'm honest, what we craved most about it was what we almost never got: Daddy's attention. He rarely took us hunting with him, but when he did, we liked having him all to ourselves.

By the time Daddy packed the old farm truck with supplies and my weepy-eyed sisters, the sun had already dipped below the horizon. Trixie chased the truck, barking her disapproval all the way to the end of the driveway.

I whispered under my breath, "I know how you feel, Trix. This ain't right."

CHAPTER 5

TURNING FROM THE HORIZON, I went inside to make supper. I wasn't much of a cook, but I knew I had to care for the family. I guess I did OK. The boys never complained about my egg and ketchup sandwiches.

At bedtime, the boys shut their door, and Ben and I spread out in the girls' room. With my sisters gone and almost the whole bed to myself, I felt like royalty. Lying in the quiet with my eyes closed, I imagined myself as a brave, magical princess who lived in the grandest castle on earth. Creatures sneaked into my room from far and wide to have slumber parties with me. They were my best friends, but only I knew about them. To keep our secret, I used my magic powers to make them disappear before my father, the king, came to tuck me in and kiss me goodnight.

As I dozed, my princess fantasy continued in a dream, with the king tucking the blankets in around my sides.

Handsome and bearded, he leaned forward and kissed my forehead. When he was done, his face glowed with delight, and I could see that he was hiding something behind his back.

He could not fight the crooked smile that gave away his secret.

"What is it, Daddy?" I asked gleefully.

The king reached behind his back and said, "This, my lovely, is the most precious gift I have ever given you."

It was a stunning purple box tied with a white ribbon.

Almost in a single motion, I undid the ribbon and opened the box. Poised on a cushion of white silk was a silver pendant studded with jewels in every color that formed the letters of my name: *J-e-s-s-i-e.*

How safe I felt! And how my heart leapt! I pulled the pendant off the silken cushion and held it to my chest.

"Thank you, Daddy! This is the most precious gift I have ever received."

Then suddenly he was gone, and an icy breeze flowed from where he had been. It blew against my face cruelly, driving back my hair and causing the candle to flicker and die out.

In the darkness, I clutched the pendant even more tightly, every ounce of my joy quickly displaced by dread. Just as quickly, the breeze departed, leaving behind a foul presence that crept close to the ground. I knew it was in the room but exactly where, I could not tell. So I sat in terror, holding my jeweled name in both hands.

In my dream, I realized that the dark presence had come only after I opened Daddy's gift. It seemed clear that the gift was what the presence was after.

I wondered where Daddy went and, with great anxiety, I expected something terrible to happen.

And it did! A wolf-like creature leapt on top of me with a terrifying roar, its face inches from mine. I could see only its pointed ears and awful yellow eyes. Its breath was rancid and hot against my skin. It squealed in a grotesquely unmusical way and clawed at my hands, trying to pry them apart.

I held my treasure tightly as the beast growled with such volume and rage that I felt dizzy. Still, I refused to release the pendant.

The harder the monster worked to have its way, the louder its wails became and the more fearsome its appearance. When I felt I could bear it no longer, my dream released me from its grip. I awoke to the sound of my own cries for help and another, more welcome sound.

"Jessie?"

"Mom!"

I fled my room and ran into the kitchen where Mom sat, still in her waitress uniform. Relieved and exhausted, I melted into her arms.

"Oh Jessie. Was it a bad dream?"

"It was awful, Mom," I sobbed.

She held me tightly, rocking back and forth and humming a beautiful melody. Waves of peace rushed over me. It was the peace I had experienced while hiding in the hollowed-out log. It seemed like long ago, but it was scarcely twenty-four hours since the strange man sang the tune Mom was humming now—the melody I sang as I gathered eggs that morning.

My sobbing ended, and I asked, "Mom, how do you know that song?"

"What song, baby?"

"The one you're singing."

Mom seemed confused. "I...I'm just making it up in my own heart."

"It's just..." I stopped myself from saying anything more. What could I possibly say? I was too exhausted to think or explain anyway.

Mom sang the song again, and I drifted off to sleep.

I slept deeply and awoke to a disorienting quiet in our house. Mom was asleep instead of in the kitchen. Daddy wasn't there to demand his eggs. And my sisters weren't there to fight over the bathroom.

All morning, I hoped for a normal school day. By recess, my hopes were dashed in the best possible way: I dethroned Ashley as the school's tetherball champion.

How good it felt to win and to be distracted from the turmoil at home!

Jake and I celebrated my victory with high-fives as Ashley begged for a rematch. Then Jake pivoted to our competition with one another. "You might be the tetherball queen, Jess, but I can still outrun you any day of the week."

"Oh yeah, Jake? You think so?"

Determined to extend my moment of glory, I challenged him to a sprint across the playground. Before we left our marks, a hand touched my shoulder.

"Congratulations, Jessie! I hear we have a new tetherball champion," Mr. Carter said, smiling from ear to ear.

"Yes sir," Jake exclaimed. "It was awesome!"

"Well, good." Mr. Carter answered Jake but stared at me. "Jessie is a talented little girl!"

My cheeks turned red hot as Mr. Carter continued. "I wonder, Jessie, if you would help me with something."

How I could help the principal, I did not know. But I was flattered to be asked. "Sure. Yes sir!"

Mr. Carter kept his hand on my shoulder. His touch felt fatherly and warm. Jake noticed and took off, sensing that he was no longer part of the conversation.

Pulling a red sucker from his pocket, Mr. Carter launched into the details of the project. In his best Texan drawl, he said, "Miss Carson needs some of her summer preschool supplies from up in the attic—you know, toys and blocks and things. I need your help to pull them down and get them washed up. Miss Langford said it would be no problem if you missed some of your afternoon class and helped me for a bit. So what do you say, Jessie?"

My heart soared so high at his invitation that I forgot to answer his question. I was overwhelmed by having defeated Ashley and having been handpicked by Mr. Carter all in one day. It was enough to turn any kid upside down. We were halfway to the school entrance when Mr. Carter paused and looked down at me—not into my eyes but down around my neck.

"So, Jessie, will you help me for a little while?"

I took his hand and continued toward the door. "Of course, Mr. Carter!"

Mr. Carter led me through the hallway to a door I had never seen opened before. It was different from most of the doors at school; this one had no windows. I'd always imagined that it hid a janitor's closet or some other eyesore. But when Mr. Carter opened it, I realized that it concealed a more interesting secret—an old wooden staircase that led to the attic.

"Here we are!" said Mr. Carter, switching on the lights and holding the door open with one hand.

As I started up the stairs, the door slammed shut, and Mr. Carter followed behind me. When we reached the attic, he switched on another light, revealing row after row of wooden shelves crammed with files, books, and all sorts of curious, broken, and useless items.

"The school district doesn't like us to throw things out," Mr. Carter explained. "Most of this stuff is nothing more than dust and rats' nests, but we have to keep it."

To me, the assortment of odds and ends was pure paradise. I walked the rows, running my hands over canvas-covered encyclopedias and other books. Mr. Carter gave me a couple of minutes to explore the place, then led me to the preschool section, where everything Miss Carson needed was on the very top shelf.

Mr. Carter positioned an old ladder for whomever would do the climbing. I hoped it would be me.

He seemed to know what I was thinking. "Jessie, do you want to go up there and hand those things down to me?"

"Sure! I'm good on ladders."

"And I'll bet you're not a bit afraid of heights, either."

"No sir. Not a bit."

I climbed the ladder, positively giddy to be inside an attic none of the other kids knew existed! Mr. Carter held his hand on my lower back as I climbed. Then, one at a time, I lowered dusty tubs of supplies into his arms. Within minutes, everything Miss Carson needed was off the shelf and ready to be cleaned.

Climbing down the ladder and clapping the dust off my hands, I thought about what a great day it was. Mr.

Carter and I worked so well together. Maybe I could help him with other things, or even be a teacher in his school someday. I was sure Miss Carson would be pleased with what we accomplished. She might even send me home with a treat or a thank-you note that I could show to Mom.

Feeling like my life had changed for the better, I asked, "What's next, Mr. Carter?" Where do we go to wash this stuff?"

His face looked blank, as though he had no idea what I was asking. The fun atmosphere became charged with nervous energy and, before I could figure out the cause, Mr. Carter rested his hands on my shoulders and kissed me on my mouth.

Falling back into the ladder and quickly recovering my balance, I looked into Mr. Carter's face. He was smiling.

"Jessie, I…"

I couldn't bear to listen. Strange information and emotions flooded my mind. My body was wracked by waves of alarm and confusion. I wasn't sure what I was supposed to say to the smiling man in front of me, so I did the only thing I knew to do: I ran—down the stairs, through the heavy door, and into the sunlight.

I scanned the playground for Jake, but there was no one. I kept running until the trees surrounded me and made me feel safe. Trees are so strong and predictable. They never change their minds or make you wonder. Trees are always right where you left them, no matter how long it's been. And whatever happens to you—however ugly or scary it is—a tree is still a tree.

For the rest of the school day, I stayed far enough in the woods to remain hidden but close enough to hear the last bell and catch the bus home. I told no one about the attic. Pretending that nothing happened seemed like the safest plan. I guess Mr. Carter felt the same way. There were no more brightly colored suckers or Jolly Ranchers. For the rest of the school year, nothing but awkwardness passed between us.

When the bell rang for the last time, I breathed a sigh of relief and burst through the school doors feeling triumphant. I had survived the troubles at home and Mr. Carter's awful kiss. There would be weeks of fun ahead, especially for Jake and me. We'd keep digging the hole, but we'd have plenty of grand adventures in the woods too.

Little did I know that the breaking of my heart had barely begun. The next few weeks would be so life-altering that I would never again walk through the doors of Lady Bird Johnson Elementary School.

CHAPTER 6

→—·—←

JAKE AND I DECIDED to spend the first week of summer vacation digging the hole for the fruit cellar. That way, we'd have the remaining weeks to do nothing but play in the woods and around the barn. The plan worked almost perfectly. After several long days and lots of blisters, we led Daddy outside to show him our masterpiece.

Daddy barely looked at us or the hole. Instead of bragging about the work we did, he walked away without a word. The all-important fruit cellar no longer seemed to matter. He had moved on. Now all he ever thought about was going hunting with Katherine and Daisy. I figured he had a manly urge to fill the freezer with stores of deer meat. Maybe it was his way to make up for not working.

Doing all that hunting wasn't Mom's idea. While she was out working, she expected Daddy to look after us and go canvassing for jobs. Instead, he went into the woods for hours and even days at a time—and never brought home a single kill. Obviously, Katherine and Daisy were no help at all. From the beginning, they complained about having to go with Daddy. At least they quit complaining after awhile.

I had a lot on my mind that summer, but I noticed some things. My sisters didn't laugh as much as they used to. They never curled their hair or dressed up in Mom's heels anymore. They didn't play with her makeup, either. When they weren't away with Daddy, they just dawdled inside, looking at picture books or daydreaming out the window. And when they returned from hunting trips, I thought I detected something inexplicable in their eyes.

It was not a happy summer, but we managed to have fun, especially when all of us kids were together. Even when there was nothing to do adventures happened, like the day Trixie summoned us to the barn with an outburst of frantic barking. All of us ran to see, including Ben.

"I bet she found a rats' nest!" Jason shouted as we ran.

By the time we got within fifty yards of Trixie, we knew she had found more than a rats' nest. She had a rattlesnake cornered and wound up tight, his rattle buzzing loudly.

Jake screamed, "No, Trixie! No! Get away from there, girl. Come here, right now!"

Trixie ignored Jake, so Jason pulled a stick off a tree and threw it for her to fetch. But even a good stick would not distract her.

Finally, Jake mustered the courage to get close and grab her collar. He then marched her back into the house and slammed the door shut. Feeling like the man of the hour, he ordered the rest of us to stand back while he decided how to kill the snake.

Jake could have asked Daddy what to do, but that would have spoiled the adventure. Instead, he decided to douse the snake in gasoline and toss a match to light it up. I thought it was a terrible idea, but I was as curious as the boys were. So I went inside to find some matches.

I checked the pantry and all the usual places. I found nothing but empty shelves, some dust, and one jar of stewed tomatoes. Suddenly the snake seemed like the least of our problems. There was no food in the house, not even enough for the next meal.

I set aside my worry for a moment, but only because I knew my brothers were waiting. I went into the living room to ask Daddy. I found him sitting as still as a stone and watching a fly buzz around the window seal. With the usual caution, I asked, "Daddy, do we have any matches?"

Fixated on the fly, he said, "I don't think."

"Umm…Daddy…where's all our food?" I knew I was pushing the envelope, but I wanted an answer.

Daddy turned to me, not with rage but with the weary hazel eyes that made Mom want to help him years earlier. Now I wanted to curl up in his lap.

"Baby, there ain't no matches. There ain't no job. There ain't no money." He moved slightly in his chair. "That means there ain't no food, either."

He seemed exhausted. "Go check the peaches."

"OK, Daddy."

It was the first real conversation we'd had in a long time. It felt so good to talk that it hurt to walk away.

I returned to the barn to find Jake and Jason parading the now headless snake. Katherine and Daisy were clearly disgusted. I was relieved that, by the grace of God, Jake had not found any gasoline, and I never found a match.

With the rattler dead, peach picking became the perfect thing for us girls to do—not because the peaches were ripe (they weren't) but because gathering them would help my sisters and me forget about the headless snake. Better still, eating them would be better than going to bed hungry.

"Hey Kat, let's grab the baskets and go check the peaches. You too, Daisy."

They were clearly relieved, grabbing the baskets before I could blink.

By the time our peach-picking was done, Mom came home from work. I was relieved to see her, especially with sacks of groceries in her arms. My sisters and I

showered her with hugs and kisses and helped her carry
the food into the house, while the boys marched around
the place showing off their bloody trophy.

"You get that filthy thing outside, and get in the tub,
now!" Mom scolded, trying not to crack a smile.

At exactly five-thirty, two squeaky clean boys and one
toddler took their seats at the table with us girls. Daddy
ambled from the living room holding a beer in one hand
and tossing three smashed empties into the trash with
the other.

From the stove Mom called out, "Daisy and Jason!
Will you two fill everyone's glasses with water, please?"

"I want milk," Jason whined.

"I'm sorry, honey. There's no milk tonight."

Daddy said, "Give the boy a beer," and flopped himself down at the head of the table.

His words were slurred, but he was serious. He
slammed down a full beer can next to Jason's plate and
said, "There you go, son. Have yourself some of that!"

"Robert! Don't even joke that way. Jason is a good boy.
He doesn't want any of that...that...poison in his system."

I closed my eyes as my mind screamed, *Stop! Don't do
it, Mom!* Then I held my breath and braced for a rampage.

Amazingly, Daddy did nothing but empty the beer down his throat. Then he belched obnoxiously, crushed the can in one hand, and tossed it over his shoulder.

Mom ignored him and served up dinner. She didn't do it in the usual way. She meted out the portions herself and handed each of us a plate. I knew what she was doing. She was trying to make a little go a long way. Each plate had a slice of white bread, two or three fried Vienna sausages cut lengthwise to look like more, and a small pile of mostly green peach slices.

"That's it?" Daddy barked.

Mom explained why our portions were limited. Some of the groceries she brought home were set aside for Sunday dinner. Daddy never let us go to church, but Mom stuck to her Methodist roots by serving big Sunday suppers.

"It's for Sunday, is it? Well, I'm a grown man every day, Donna. A. Grown. Man."

Daddy's eyes bulged as he stretched out his words, seemingly for shock value. "I don't know of any woman in Jefferson County who would give baby food to a grown man. No woman in Texas would disrespect her husband like that."

"And I don't know of any man in Texas who cries about being hungry but refuses to get a job—and can't even kill a single deer."

"Mom..."

Jake aborted his warning, knowing the damage had already been done. Jason knew it too and quickly took refuge in the boys' room. I froze in my seat, afraid to leave Mom with Daddy. He was like a keg of gunpowder, and her remark was more than enough to ignite him.

Daddy's neck and face turned scarlet. He stood up slowly, seeming to enjoy the drama. He knew Mom was afraid of him, but he also knew she would not run. She simply closed her eyes and braced for the blow.

When Daddy delivered, Mom fell to her knees. Then he yanked her long hair, snapping her head back and forcing her back to her feet.

"Stop, Robert! Stop!"

Mom groaned in pain and repeated her plea, which only fueled more violence. Daddy continued dragging her by the hair, all the way into their bedroom.

When he slammed their door shut, Jake screamed, "Stop! *Stop!*"

Utter helplessness compelled Jake to run out the side door again. My sisters and I remained at the table with Ben, who poked at a Vienna sausage with his tiny index finger. The rest of us had barely touched our food. All of us lost our appetites. Katherine collected our plates and scraped their contents into a Tupperware bowl. She clanked the fork with each stroke, turned the faucet on high, and noisily piled plates in the sink. It wasn't enough to drown out the sounds issuing from Mom and Daddy's room.

Daisy walked out the side door. I followed her a minute or two later. She was sitting on the cool concrete step, hugging her knees to her chest. A deep sorrow and brokenness seemed to rush from her soul and out through the crystal blue of her irises. I was sure there was a secret she wanted to tell. So I sat on the step and hugged my knees too.

"You OK, Daisy?"

Tears trailed down her cheeks. She was not OK—not at all. She tried to sniff back the mess that reached her upper lip but rubbed it on her arm instead. Slightly repulsed, I pulled a tissue from my pocket and pushed against the step to stand up. When I did, I realized that on this bone-dry day, the concrete under Daisy's bottom was warmly soaked, along with the backside of her dress.

"Come on, sissy," I said calmly. "Let's get you a nice warm bath."

We didn't see Mom or Daddy again that night. After my sisters were asleep, I lay on our mattress with my eyes closed, searching for the melody of the strange man in the woods. I wondered who he was and why his song affected me so deeply. I wondered where he was now and why he was in the woods the night I hid in the log. I wished he was with me now.

After awhile, part of his melody bubbled up from my memory and wrapped my heart in peace. I hummed it until I fell sleep.

I don't recall anything more about that night, but Mom told me many times that she and Daddy woke up to find me rummaging through their dresser, searching underneath folded articles of clothing.

"What are you doing, Jessie?" asked Mom.

"I'm looking for the savior."

"You sure as hell won't find him here," Daddy growled.

"I have to find his song," I whimpered while sleep-walking back to my room.

It's impossible to say exactly what I was thinking. Looking back, I believe my young heart yearned for the man who was unlike any I had ever met—the man who knew me like no one else did.

Yet Daddy was right: there was no savior in that house. If there had been, he would surely have rescued us from the pain of that night or whisked us away to some happier place, wouldn't he?

If only he had, the event that would soon end my childhood might never have happened.

CHAPTER 7

"ONE, TWO, THREE, SLAM!"

We counted off and giggled each time Jake shoved another hay bale off the barn loft and onto the floor below.

"One more, y'all. Ready?"

"Go! Go! Go!" Jason whooped.

"Give me the countdown!" Jake ordered.

"One, two, three, slam!"

The last bale tumbled on top of four others, creating the perfect fort.

Playing in hay forts kept us busy all day. Before lunch, we were pirates warring among ourselves, dodging cannon balls and slashing at each other with stick swords. Jake, our captain, stood on the ship's bow commanding us to drop the sails and outrun the scurvy dogs. Then, when the scurvy dogs overran our ship, they took Daisy and Katherine captive. The girls' cries were our cue to launch a swashbuckling rescue operation using the barn

rope and pulley to swoop down and retrieve the scream-
ing damsels.

After lunch, we became Alaskan wilderness explorers
who braved arctic temperatures and polar bears for the
sake of humanity. Leaving the shelter of our igloo, Jake
and Jason killed no fewer than sixteen bears with their
machine-gun sticks. They even built an imaginary bon-
fire to cook one of the beasts for dinner.

We were so happy on that perfect summer Sunday.

While we played, I noticed Daddy loading up the old
farm truck. Now, with the sun dropping toward the horizon, he strode into the barn with his rifle slung behind
his shoulder.

"Daisy. Katherine. Let's go."

My sisters' faces drained at Daddy's request. Instead
of being brave arctic explorers, they reverted to being
the submissive daughters of an alcohol-driven father.
Without the least bit of resistance, they lined up behind
him and followed him out of the barn.

Mom appeared at that moment, flustered and slightly
out of breath. "Not this time, Robert. Sunday supper is
almost ready."

"It don't matter. I packed sandwiches."

"No, Robert. Please." Mom fiddled with her necklace
and pleaded, "Please stay home tonight."

Daddy glared at Mom for a seeming eternity, and
uncharacteristically gave up the fight.

"Y'all need to get in the house and get washed up for supper," said Daddy without emotion.

His orders surprised us so much that we forgot to move.

"Now!" he roared.

None of us would have chosen to miss this meal. It was Sunday supper at its best. I smiled across the table at Daisy, who seemed delighted to be staying home. It was as though the joy of our play time resumed in the evening. Not wanting to squander it, we older kids cleaned the kitchen promptly, leaving plenty of time for nighttime games. Mom even joined us on the living room floor, laughing and shaking the Yahtzee dice in their cup.

We had a fun evening, playing and laughing together until bedtime. Contented and fully satisfied, we girls fell asleep quickly. But sometime before morning, I was startled by something tickling my neck. I was slow to grasp what it was.

The rotten smell of whisky gave it away. I jerked my head from the mattress to find Daddy kneeling over me with his face uncomfortably close to mine.

"Daddy!" I cried.

He lurched to his feet, struggling to keep his balance.

"What are you doing in here? Are you sleepwalking?"

He didn't speak but only shuffled his feet and bobbed his head in a drunken stupor. Finally, he placed an unruly finger over his lips and muttered, "Shhh." Then he dropped to his knees again and placed one hand on my stomach.

"Daddy! What are you—"

"Shhh."

He shifted his hand.

"Daddy, stop!" I mumbled, swatting away his hand.

"You shut up and be still."

His hand shifted again.

"No!" I slapped his arm as hard as I could.

He wagged his finger in my face.

"You listen to me, Jessie. You listen! Do you hear me?"

"What?" I shouted defiantly.

"Damn you, Jessie!"

He pointed his finger, not at my face this time but my body.

"You're nothin' to nobody. Nothin' but a worthless piece of meat. A piece of damn meat, Jessie. Ain't nobody ever going to love you, so you might as well let me."

With those words, a dark night descended on my heart. I lay there speechless, staring at Daddy's hazel eyes and blaming myself for his anger. I thought of when Mr. Carter kissed me. Maybe I was a piece of meat. Mr. Carter seemed to think so. Now Daddy did too.

Suddenly Daddy broke eye contact with me and looked over at Katherine, who was awake but not moving. In the moonlight I thought I saw teardrops trailing down the side of her face, even before Daddy reached her side of the bed.

When he went to touch her, I cried, "No!"

The grit in my voice surprised him and pierced his stupor. He pulled back his hand, stood up, and huffed his way out of the room.

Katherine stared at the ceiling and wept softly. Suddenly it all made sense. The hunting trips. The funny look in Katherine's and Daisy's eyes. The way they seemed to change. The fact that they rarely laughed anymore.

"He's done that to you before?" I asked.

"Yes," whispered Katherine.

"A lot?"

"Yes."

"And worse?"

A pause.

"Yes."

"That's it, Katherine. I'm leaving."

CHAPTER 8

"YOU CAN'T LEAVE now, Jess. Not when it's the middle of the night!"

Katherine wasn't trying to change my mind. No one could have done that. Still, I was torn. Deep down I ached to fix things with Daddy. I even wished I could ignore what he did in our bedroom. But I could do neither. Nor could I stay another day. I could barely manage another minute.

My feelings for Daddy were a complicated tangle of love, longing, fear, shame, and hatred. My twelve-year-old soul had already been crushed under a lifetime of neglect and hurtful words. This new, revolting breach made the situation perfectly clear. It wasn't that I wanted to run away from Daddy. More than anything, I wanted to be held by him. But what he did and said proved that he would never hold me the way I wanted to be held. He would never be the safe place I needed him to be.

That realization was more than I could bear.

"I'll leave before the sun comes up."

"I'm coming with you."

"Are you sure, Kat?"

"I'm sure."

"OK. Let's get some sleep."

The only sleep I got came between adrenaline-soaked imaginings about what was ahead. Then Katherine's gentle tap awakened me for good. I rubbed my eyes to find her sitting on the floor with a pair of scissors in her hand and several family photo albums stacked up beside her.

"What are you doing?"

"I'm taking these with me," she said, motioning to two dozen or so photos she'd cut out.

I wanted to look at each one, but the red numbers on our alarm clock declared that it was 5:03 A.M. There was no time to reminisce. It was time to run away.

The birds were singing, but Ben and Daisy were still asleep. Trying my best to be quiet, I went out to the garage to find an empty cardboard box. On the way back to the girls' room I paused at Jake and Jason's door, which was ajar. The boys were stretched out and fast asleep on their bed. I so wanted to hug them tightly and say good-bye, but I couldn't. So I whispered my farewell and moved on.

Katherine and I packed the carton with the barest essentials: a single change of clothes, her cut-out photos, and two peaches. At the very last second, Katherine added her Barbie doll.

By the time we reached the back door, it began to rain. We argued over whether an umbrella would help us or slow us down. We decided to leave the umbrella behind, but as we exited the house, I worried that our conversation had been too loud. Before that, I was certain that everyone was asleep, but now I looked over my shoulder, feeling like someone was watching us.

Someone *was* watching, not from the house but the barn. It was Trixie. I feared that once we made eye contact with her, she would run to greet us and bark loudly enough to wake the dead.

She did exactly that.

"Trixie! No!" I exclaimed, with the strongest whisper I could muster. "Go home, Trixie. Go home!"

"You can't come with us, girl. You just can't," Katherine pleaded.

Trixie was undeterred. She whined and wagged her tail, begging to join our adventure. We loved her but could not afford any more commotion. At any moment, Daddy could wake up and realize what the hoopla was all about.

I thrust the carton into Katherine's hands and took Trixie by the collar, hoping that if I got her into the house, she would settle down. I knew there was no guarantee it would work. She might create an even bigger problem in the house. But we had only two options, and the barn option had already failed.

Trixie cooperated with me, but before I could latch the door, she began barking wildly. A cold panic sped through my veins. I raced across the yard and back to Katherine as though the devil himself was on my tail.

"Go, Kat! Run!"

We ran and ran. Katherine was not as fast or coordinated as I was. More than once, I had to slow down and let her catch up to me. For a while it felt like a game Jake and I played countless times, sprinting through the woods on some adventure or another. But this was not a fun game. Unless we covered significant ground in a hurry, we would soon find ourselves in a world of hurt.

So we ran as hard and as fast as we could. Both of us were soaked. So was the carton.

"I'll take that," I said, pulling it from Katherine's hands.

The box had no lid, so I tucked the photos and peaches all the way under the folded clothes. It didn't help all that much because the cardboard was soggy all around.

"You go straight into the woods, and I'll follow you," I told Katherine. "Just keep going toward the creek."

She took off on a girlish jog, splashing through puddles as I followed close behind. One side of the box was tearing away. The whole thing was about to come completely apart. I had to do something with it, but I had no idea what.

That's when I realized where we were. Twenty yards away, the familiar hollow log lay partially buried in the dirt. Goosebumps traveled up my arms as I remembered the comfort I'd found inside that log months earlier. I thought about the strange man in the woods and the song he sang. The melody had stuck with me ever since. Now, as I stared at the log, I heard the song in my head, as clear as ever, with the same strange words and beautiful melody filling my ears. I did not see the man this time or hear his voice. Yet I felt sure that Katherine and I were not alone.

"Hey, Jess, let's go."

Katherine's voice returned me to the strain of our current reality.

"Right," I said. "Let's go."

We were now in the middle of the forest, about half-way between our house and the school. The distance between us and Daddy gave us some comfort. So did the early hour, which I figured to be before 6:30. Even after sunrise, the heavy cloud cover would make for a dark morning. Unless Trixie's commotion had awakened him earlier, Daddy would still be dead asleep.

"Hey look at that!" said Katherine, pointing to the rusted remains of an abandoned pickup truck.

"Wow," I whispered. "How cool is that?"

The metal carcass was so corroded that the truck's original color was unknowable. The hood was up and the engine compartment was practically stripped bare. The tires were gone. So were the wheels. Of the rear end, only the frame remained, but the cab and all of the glass were still intact.

The passenger door worked perfectly. When I opened it, the smell of dust, oil, and old things filled the air. After the truck's body had rotted in the woods for who knows how many years, its interior was bone dry. I set what was left of the soggy box on the black leather bench seat and shut the door, hoping we could retrieve our things some other time.

For now we needed to go down to the creek and cross over it. That would put us out of the woods and close to the school and open pasture. On a dry day, we could have been there within minutes. But in the rain the descent through rocks and prickly pear cactus was more difficult.

We slipped and slid much of the way down until we were soaked to the bone and splattered with mud. The clear little creek we once leapt easily was now a muddy, swollen, fast-moving river. The idea of crossing it was more than intimidating.

"I don't want to go in," Katherine said, grabbing at my hand.

Wading through the creek was not an option. I scanned the bank for another way.

"Stay right here, Kat. I'll go find a log or something to get us over."

I followed the path along the water, which led to a thicket that tore at my clothes. With Katherine out of sight and the forest darkened by rain, I felt sickeningly alone and vulnerable. I realized that my resolve to get away from Daddy could not overcome the fear that now washed over me.

In my overwhelm, I heard Katherine scream my name. *Oh no. The river!*

Images of my sister being carried off by the force of the water barraged my mind.

"Katherine!" I hollered. "I'm coming!"

As I spun around, a massive black creature darted from the path behind me and disappeared into the woods. Overcome with terror, I fell backward to the ground. Whatever the beast was, it had been following me. The question was whether it was hunting me.

I knew there were not supposed to be wolves in Texas, and that most wolf sightings were actually coyotes. But the beast I saw resembled the wolf-like creature from my dream. The last thing I wanted was to encounter it up close. But I feared losing my sister even more, so I ran toward the sound of her voice.

Relief doused my fears when I found Katherine on terra firma. Never had I been so grateful to see her throwing a flat-out fit.

"We can't do this, Jessie!" She pleaded, pounding her fists on the wet ground. "We can't cross that river!"

"I know, Kat. I know. Are you OK?"

"No! I don't want to do this anymore! We have to go home—now!"

"Kat, what do you think Daddy would do to us if we went back now?"

She began to cry.

"He'd kill us, Katherine! I mean it. The other night he threatened to chop Mom into little pieces and bury her in the backyard! I heard him tell her so. Can you imagine how he would punish us for running away?"

There was truth to my argument, but I shouldn't have said those things to Katherine. She was already hysterical and did not need me fueling her fear. So I stopped talking, locked my arm in hers, and continued to search for a way across the creek.

She cried the whole time. I was as terrified as she was, but we had different ways of showing it. Katherine's emotions ran like a river. Anything hidden under the water quickly bobbed to the surface. My emotions were concealed, piled up behind the dam I built inside myself. Kat's way was probably healthier, but at least one of us needed to function. For the time being, my dam allowed me to be that one.

Katherine eventually calmed down until she slipped on a wet rock, caught her hand in a patch of prickly pear cactus, and became inconsolable again. I pulled out as many needles as I could and pleaded with her to keep moving.

She put on her brave face, and on we went. About a hundred yards from where she fell, I spotted exactly what I'd hoped to find—a fallen tree big and sturdy enough to be our bridge across the river.

With rushing waters below us, the crossing was tricky. Thank God, it was uneventful. We hopped off the far end of the fallen tree and proceeded up a steep embankment. Finally, we entered the vast open field, which was bisected by a small gravel road. On its far side was a small yellow house. Beyond the house was our school and the town of Woodcrest.

What welcome sights they were!

As I thought about what to do next, I heard an automobile approaching. "Get down!" I shouted.

We dropped on our bellies.

"Is it Daddy? Is it?" Katherine squeezed her eyes shut as if closing them would keep her from being seen.

"I don't know. I don't think so."

The car that passed within several feet of us was red.

I sighed and said, "We're OK."

We stood and looked across the field and, in a real way, toward our future. The night before, I had decided to run away—away from home, away from Daddy, away from hell on earth. Now, on the edge of someplace new and uncertain, I wondered what my sister and I were running toward.

There wasn't time to wonder for long. Another vehicle approached from a good distance down the road. We needed to cross it and take cover before that car got close enough to see us.

"Run, Kat!" I yelled, my voice cracking. "Run!"

CHAPTER 9

WE COULD NOT RISK being spotted, even if the approaching driver was a perfect stranger. Any adult would wonder why two girls were alone on the roadside at that hour. The last thing we needed was a good Samaritan helping us to get home. So Katherine and I summoned whatever speed was left in our legs to get across the road and out of sight.

A shocking surprise greeted us on the other side: a makeshift barbed wire fence that neither of us had noticed. Now there was no turning back. The only route to some semblance of safety was forward.

"There's enough room under the bottom wire, Kat. Just shimmy under it."

We slid onto the muddy ground and cleared the fence safely, but it slowed us down. I had no idea who lived in the yellow house ahead, but I convinced myself that if we ran toward it, the oncoming driver would assume that we lived there—unless, of course, that driver was Daddy.

The car passed behind us. I turned to see that it was a white sedan. I was relieved, until I heard a squeal of brakes.

The car stopped. The driver was watching.

"Stop running, Kat. Take my hand."

"What if they know us?"

"Just keep walking."

We pretended to walk casually around the side of the house. A few more steps would place us out of sight. With our hearts pounding, we stepped onto the manicured section of lawn nearest the house and waited until we heard the sound of tires kicking up gravel. The white car went on its way.

Katherine threw her arms around me and squeezed me tightly.

"I think we're safe, Jess. Do you?"

"I think so," I replied, "but do you know who lives here?"

"It's a lady and her kids. I'm pretty sure they're from our school."

"Do they know Mom and Daddy? Do we know her kids?"

Katherine shrugged.

Having made it this far, I decided that knocking on the lady's door couldn't be terribly scary. I took my sister's hand again, walked with her up the cement steps, and pushed the doorbell. A dog yapped wildly to announce our arrival.

With two clicks, the door was unlocked, and a girl younger than either of us pulled it open. She was half asleep and still in her nightgown, with her hair going every which way. As she stared in silence, her frenetic little dog inspected every inch of us.

"Is your mom home?" I asked, trying not to sound as weird as I imagined we looked.

"Who's there, honey?" a soft voice inquired from inside the house.

The girl's mother appeared almost instantaneously. She was beautiful, with auburn hair falling in lovely waves past her shoulders. Across her nose and cheeks a perfect patch of freckles matched her hair. She looked like a mom from a magazine. She was even wearing a dress and apron, like magazine moms wore.

"Can I help you?" she asked with a measured sense of alarm.

Katherine and I burst into tears.

What a shock it must have been for the red-haired mom! By now we looked like children from a savage, far-away kingdom who dropped into the civilized world by accident. At least it felt that way to me. The environment we landed in was completely foreign. It was warm and clean and the air smelled sweet. The beauty of it made me sob even harder.

"Oh, honeys, come on in," the mom swooned. "Let's get you dry. Then we will figure out how to get you home, OK?"

Katherine turned to me in terror, knowing that if the nice lady sent us home, we were as good as dead.

Two boys peeked out from the living room. Then all three of the children who belonged in the yellow house retreated to the couch and continued staring at us. Who could blame them?

Their mom returned with two fluffy towels and draped one over each of our heads.

"What are your names?" she asked.

We returned nothing but blank stares.

"My name is Rhonda, or Ms. Wilson, if you prefer."

"Hi," Katherine said shyly.

I wasn't feeling shy. I was scared and knew that if I didn't speak up, things would go badly for us.

"We're not lost," I declared.

"I'm sorry?" Ms. Wilson seemed taken aback by my abrupt, almost clinical response.

"We aren't lost."

Ms. Wilson cleared her throat. "Can I ask why you're here so early in the morning? And why you're soaked in rain and mud? And why there are cactus needles in your sister's hand?"

I felt sobs rising from deep in my belly again.

Ms. Wilson continued, "And why you are so frightened?"

She waited for an answer, but none came. She looked straight at me, not in a threatening way but an imploring one. "Honey, what is your name?"

"Jessie. My sister's name is Katherine."

For years I'd felt the weight of the Jenkins' family secret. At the thought of exposing it, I collapsed in Ms. Wilson's arms.

She didn't ask any more questions. Instead, she comforted me. Then she went to the kitchen and made breakfast while Katherine and I sat on the living room floor watching Scooby Doo cartoons with her kids.

I had not noticed how hungry I was until the smell of bacon and eggs started my stomach growling. Mercifully, Ms. Wilson appeared from around the corner and smiled. "Girls, your breakfast is ready. Come sit at the table."

Ms. Wilson told her children to take their plates to their rooms, saying, "Mommy, Jessie, and Katherine need to talk for a little bit, OK?"

The children filed out of the kitchen stiffly, each one carrying a heaping plate with both hands.

Arranged side by side on the table were two of the most beautifully heaped breakfast plates I'd ever seen. Each held a steaming mound of scrambled eggs, three slices of bacon, two slices of toast with butter and jam, and a whole pile of peach slices—not green ones from the yard but the sweet ones you get from a can.

Ms. Wilson smiled as I shoveled some eggs onto my fork. Katherine (always the lady) thanked our hostess before taking her first bite.

"You are most welcome, sweetie," Ms. Wilson replied. "Go ahead and eat, both of you!"

There was a lot more to take in than good food. Being in a cozy house with the lovely Ms. Wilson captivated me. My intense fear all but melted away. Ms. Wilson must have sensed that I had lowered my guard, because she started asking questions again.

"So, where do you girls live?"

"Across the field, on the other side of the forest," Katherine replied.

"You're Jenkins kids?"

I searched her eyes, hoping to read her intentions before I answered.

"Yes," I muttered, looking at my lap.

"And you did say that you're not lost, right?"

We nodded.

"Well honeys, I'm trying to understand why two sweet little girls would show up on my doorstep weeping. Your home is miles away. School is closed. Yet you came all the way here." She leaned forward and whispered knowingly, "Either something was chasing you, or something is all out of sorts at home."

"Home is fine," I lied.

Katherine burst into tears, betraying my deceit. I wondered why I'd lied in the first place.

"Jessie, you can tell me."

I honestly didn't know what to say. Too many thoughts raced through my mind: *Daddy is a monster and he hates me. Daddy is a drunk. Daddy broke Jake's nose. Daddy whipped my baby brother. Daddy hurts Mom and says he will kill her. Daddy tried to touch me. And Mr. Carter...*

My head spun until I thought it would explode. "Everything is wrong!" I screamed.

Ms. Wilson's response was unreserved. Her arms enveloped me, and she pulled me close to her chest, rocking me back and forth as I cried.

"Oh, Jessie."

Now she was crying and struggling to speak. "It's OK, honey. You're here with me and you're safe. You girls are going to be OK."

We rocked gently until the tsunami of sorrow ebbed and we could communicate again.

"Tell me about your daddy, Katherine."

Obviously, Ms. Wilson had heard enough talk around town to know which questions to ask. "He's an oil man, right?"

"Yes ma'am," Katherine said sheepishly, "but he lost his job, and now he's home all the time."

"Is he a good daddy?

Before either of us could answer, Ms. Wilson rephrased her question and looked at Katherine.

"Is he nice to you kids?"

Katherine looked away. "Sort of, I guess." Then she turned back and confessed, "Not always."

"Does he ever get angry, Katherine?"

"Yes."

"Does he drink beer a lot?"

"Yes."

"Is that when he gets angry?"

I answered before Katherine opened her mouth. "He's always drinking beer or whatever. And he's always angry."

Ms. Wilson paid close attention to my every word, which emboldened me to say more.

"And sometimes when he drinks, he acts weird."

Ms. Wilson tilted her head. "What do you mean, Jessie?"

"About what?" I asked.

"What does your daddy do that's weird?"

"He yells at us. He spanks us. He hits us with the stick. He…"

I paused to make sure I wanted to say what came next.

"He broke my brother's nose."

Ms. Wilson's hands went to her mouth in disbelief.

"I'm so sorry, honey. Is your brother OK now?"

"Yeah," I said matter-of-factly, "that was like a month ago."

Ms. Wilson leaned in close and lowered her eyes, as if to show respect. "Does your father ask you to do grownup things with him?"

"What do you mean?"

At first I didn't understand what Ms. Wilson was talking about. Then she turned to Katherine, who knew exactly what she meant.

Katherine nodded her head in shame. Ms. Wilson reached across the table, placing her hand on Katherine's arm.

"I'm so sorry, baby."

She said it as sincerely as I had ever heard anyone say anything, and she started to cry again.

"That's not OK," said Ms. Wilson.

A stubborn resolve gripped her freckled face as she stood up from the table, dabbed her eyes, and sent Katherine and me back to the living room to watch television. I heard her make a phone call, but I could only make out bits and pieces of the conversation. I assumed she was talking to the police. She gave our names, whispered a few details through her tears, then repeated her address twice to the person on the other end of the line.

When she hung up, I wondered what would happen next. The thought of the police coming over scared me. I feared that Katherine and I might be in trouble for stealing pictures out of the family albums.

The doorbell rang minutes after Ms. Wilson hung up the phone. I thought, *The police are here already?*

Ms. Wilson peeked out the window, then turned to Katherine and me looking like she'd seen a ghost. "Girls, you need to lock yourselves in the bathroom and stay there until I tell you to come out."

Ms. Wilson's once calm voice was now vibrating. So were her hands.

When I stood up from the couch and glimpsed out the window, I knew why. Daddy's blue pickup was in the driveway.

CHAPTER 10

"IT'S DADDY! HE'S HERE!"

I yanked Katherine through the bathroom door and struggled to lock it.

"What are you doing, Jess?"

"The lock is stuck."

"Forget the lock! You're making a racket."

Kat was right about the noise, but hiding in an unlocked bathroom seemed like a bad idea. So I tried again and finally locked the thing. Then the two of us slipped behind the shower curtain and pressed our ears against the bathroom wall. The conversation from the living room was muffled, but Ms. Wilson definitely wasn't speaking to Daddy.

"Mrs. Jenkins, right?"

"Yes, Donna Jenkins," said Mom. "I'm sorry to bother you Mrs.—"

"Ms. Wilson."

"I'm sorry...Ms. Wilson...but our oldest girls, Jessie and Katherine, have gone missing."

"Oh no! Where do you think—I mean—could they be out playing somewhere?"

"No. Not before breakfast. I'm so worried. Their dad and the other kids are looking in the woods...but..."

Mom sounded too weary to finish her sentence. An awkward silence preceded Ms. Wilson's response.

"I'm so sorry, Mrs. Jenkins. I—here—let me get you a tissue."

Hearing Mom's sobs and Ms. Wilson's well-intended lies was almost unbearable, but we kept quiet. It was harder for Katherine than it was for me. The strain turned her face a deep shade of scarlet, and her eyes betrayed her broken heart. Emotionally exhausted, she plopped down on the edge of the tub.

I continued listening through the wall.

"I don't think I know your girls. Do you—"

"Oh, yes. Of course. Here's a snapshot. That's Katherine. She's ten. It's hard to tell in black and white, but her hair and eyes are brown. And that's my twelve-year-old, Jessie. She's dirty blond, with lots of freckles."

Mom broke down again. "She's so beautiful! They're both so beautiful!"

Mom's words crushed me. I lay down in the tub and wept with Katherine, who cried under her breath, "Mommy. Mommy. *Mom-my.*"

I felt like the lowest, cruelest person on earth. Not only had I broken Mom's heart by leaving, but I stayed silent as she suffered in the next room. How I wanted to throw myself into her arms and tell her I was sorry!

Katherine apparently felt the same way. She leapt to her feet, threw open the shower curtain, and lunged toward the door. I caught her by the back of her shirt, but just barely.

"No, Kat! Don't!"

"I'm going with Mommy!" she said, in anything but a whisper.

I pulled her to my chest and covered her mouth forcefully. "Stop it, Kat. Please stop."

Too distraught to cooperate, Katherine fought to get free. Unwilling to return to Daddy, I fought harder, pinning down my own sister and pressing my hand so hard against her mouth, it's a wonder she could breathe.

As we both reached the end of our strength, we heard a car door slam and an engine turn over. Mom was driving away, without her girls.

Ms. Wilson opened the bathroom door, which apparently had never locked. "It's OK, girls." She was clearly heartsick, as any mother would have been.

Poor Katherine stumbled to the couch, where she sat and bawled. Within moments, another vehicle appeared in the driveway. This one had red and blue lights on top.

There's no going back now, Jessie.

The thought was much heavier than I expected.

CHAPTER 11

THE SAME POLICEMEN who talked with Katherine and me later told Mom and Daddy that we were all right but would not be coming home. They left us at kind Ms. Wilson's house that night, but the next day, another nice lady drove us a hundred miles away, to a home in Beaumont, Texas. There we met our foster parents, Adam and Beth Barnes. Katherine and I naturally called them Mr. Barnes and Mrs. Barnes. They insisted that we call them Adam and Beth.

Months after leaving Woodcrest and settling in with the Barnes family, I sat at the piano piecing together the tune sung by the man in the woods. I remembered only a handful of notes, but when I strung them together, they were enough to take me back.

G - A - B - G - C - B - A...

G - A - B - G - C - B - A...

G - A - B - G - C - B - A.

The song was beautiful. The more I played it, the more I realized that it was part of my life story, which wasn't beautiful at all. At twelve, I already led a complicated life. I saw violence at home. I was far from my parents. I missed my mother, my sister Daisy, and my brothers. I wondered whether I would see any of them ever again. It was quite a story, and none of us could escape it.

Adam and Beth were nice folks, but they weren't *my* folks. And neither of them knew how to cook. Beth cooked anyway, but the food was never appetizing. She even made Sunday supper, but it was nothing like Mom's. By the time we got home from church, I was so hungry that her bad cooking disappointed me even more.

To the Barnes's credit we went to church every Sunday. It was not at all what I expected, and it required a fair amount of effort. Beth helped Katherine and me squeeze into pretty dresses and pulled back our hair into painfully tight ponytails. As if that weren't enough, she curled our bangs and locked in the curl with a coat of hairspray.

At church, we sat in the pew with Beth and Adam until the sermon was over. Then Katherine and I would head down to the kids' classroom where we'd sit around tables, listen to Bible stories, and cut up pieces of colored paper. We'd glue those pieces together to make crosses, arks, and mangers from the stories we read.

I admit that church was great fun. Learning about people like Noah, Goliath, and Jonah was new to me. I heard their stories and about how God saw them and even talked to some of them. It made me look at my own life differently: I realized that other people—even great people—had tough lives. I wondered whether they had ever heard the song I heard in the woods.

Although I wondered, I never asked.

Adam was what the people at church called an elder. Everyone acted like he was important, so I figured that he was a leader. That meant doing important things like passing the offering buckets, which he did every Sunday. Several times I heard people tell him how proud they were to have Adam and Beth in the county's emergency foster care program. Right in front of me, one man told Adam, "It must be hard taking in troubled children. But I know the Lord will give you the strength."

I didn't think that Katherine and I were that much trouble.

Adam and Beth did deserve credit for helping kids like us. Between Katherine and me and their own children, Susan and Adam Jr., they had a full house. When we first arrived in Beaumont, Susan seemed very welcoming, taking time to show us her doll collection and inviting us to play in her room. Adam Jr. was already in high school, but he showed us around the property, pointing out all the fun places to play and warning us about the rattlesnakes under the back deck.

Things started out well, but after a few months Susan grew tired of sharing her parents' affection with strangers. Adam Jr. got bored with us as time went on, but at least he wasn't hostile.

One afternoon, when Katherine and I were having fun in the backyard, Beth called us inside to sit at the kitchen table with her. We obeyed quickly and were surprised to find bowls of vanilla ice cream with drizzled chocolate syrup awaiting us. Katherine dove right in, but I hesitated. I wondered what kind of bad news was coming.

"Girls..." she began.

OK, I thought. *Here we go.*

"I have some news to share about your family. I think you'll be very excited about some of it, but you probably won't like all of it."

Beth finished her sentence and smiled at us. I wasn't sure what kind of reaction she was expecting, but neither Katherine nor I smiled back.

"OK," said Beth. "Let's start with the tough part." She furrowed her brow in what seemed like a rehearsed expression of sympathy.

"The police went to your parents' house this morning."

I was not ready for that.

"They talked with your mom and dad and your siblings. They explained that you girls are happy and doing very well. After talking with the family, they felt it was best—now here's the good news—"

Beth smiled like it was Christmas morning. I thought I was going to throw up.

"Daisy is coming!"

"When?" Katherine squealed.

"Today. She's coming *today!*"

Katherine was ecstatic. I was traumatized. "What time will she be here?" was all I could ask.

"She could be here any time," said Beth. "And she's going to be so excited to see you two!"

While Beth and Katherine celebrated, I wondered what the real story was. I was thrilled to hear that I'd see Daisy again. But I had questions about what was going on at home. Daisy had obviously not run away. So why was she being separated from the family?

"Are they taking Daddy to jail?"

"No Jess, they aren't."

Beth seemed miffed, as though my lack of enthusiasm had destroyed her carefully planned moment. "They will probably revisit that issue in a few weeks. But the wonderful news right now is that Daisy is coming to live with us!"

Daisy arrived less than an hour later and immediately transferred her three sets of clothes from a cardboard box to the dresser that Katherine and I already shared. We were so happy to see her that we smothered her with hugs. Our reunion was wonderful, but I could not shake the guilt I carried for running away and messing up the family. I apologized to Daisy repeatedly. She said she didn't blame me for anything that happened, but the guilt would not let me go.

I figured Daisy had emotions of her own to struggle with. While Katherine and I adjusted to a new life, she was at home for the chaos and trauma that followed the splitting of the family. There was probably talk about Daddy going to jail and worry about the rest of the family falling apart. Now, with Daisy in foster care, the family took another blow. I imagined their sorrow at seeing Daisy removed from home. And poor Daisy! She had to look each family member in the eye and say good-bye. That would be enough to make any kid a wreck.

Yet Daisy seemed perfectly calm, at least on the outside. Even as we bombarded her with questions about everyone and everything at home, she remained subdued, ignoring most of them and quietly adjusting to her new surroundings. She did address our main concern: she said the family was "fine" and there hadn't been any more big blowups.

No sooner had Daisy finished putting away her things and checking out her new bedroom than she and Katherine began playing, just like old times. They were close in age and had always been inseparable. Now they were smiling again. I was happy for them; but it was hard on me. As time went on, they grew even closer, doing the girly things they loved most, like painting their nails and playing pretend games about princes and princesses. While they giggled, I wandered around alone, missing my buddy Jake.

It was a lonely time for me. Susan, whose jealousy increased with Daisy's arrival, regularly played dolls with Daisy and Katherine. No one ever invited me. Not that playing dolls was my thing. It wasn't. But it hurt to be excluded and to realize that having more of my family in Beaumont meant spending more time alone, not less.

Staring out the window became one of my pastimes. I thought about all kinds of things, especially things over which I had no control, like what was going on at home and whether anyone was taking care of the chickens. I fretted about Mom and Jake. And Ben. And Jason. I daydreamed about my Daddy and revisited the incident with Mr. Carter. I thought about men in general, even the man in the woods. I didn't understand what it all meant; I only knew that my feelings about these men were inseparable from the deep, empty pit that existed somewhere in my insides.

In retrospect, I can see that Beth recognized my increasing isolation. One day, she gave me several sheets of yellow construction paper and a handful of crayons.

She encouraged me to "make something beautiful that will make us all feel happy," and she promised that if I did a really good job, she would display my masterpiece on the refrigerator.

Making everyone happy did not seem like something I was equipped to do, but I accepted the challenge and went to work. I wasn't much of an artist. At best, I had average skills for a girl my age. But I worked at the drawing and took my time. I began by drawing myself. Then I drew a trail, so it looked like I was walking on it. It was exactly the kind of trail I liked; it was surrounded by trees. The more I focused on the scene, the prettier it became. I even imagined it hanging on the fridge for everyone to see.

Just when my picture seemed almost perfect, a new vein of inspiration opened up. It was different from what I'd done so far. Instead of bright colors, I chose the black crayon and drew a familiar shadow with pointy ears and a tail—the wolf I'd seen in my dream, the same creature that appeared when Katherine and I escaped through the woods. In my drawing, the wolf lurked behind a tree, watching me.

After the wolf was finished, I added the sun and several shades of green to the grass and tree branches. The bottom corner of the paper was still blank, so I drew a half circle and colored in a sky blue lake. Then I decided that more people needed to be in the picture. I didn't like the way it looked with me and the wolf alone in the woods. Almost without thinking, I drew a man standing a few steps behind me on the path near the lake. When I finished coloring in his hair, face, and clothing, I laid down my crayon and studied the scene. It was so real to me that I easily imagined myself being in it.

Just then, yet another wave of inspiration flowed from the depths of my broken twelve-year-old heart. Sifting through the pile of crayons, I selected a brown and a gold one. First I added a handsome brown beard to the man standing behind me. Then, using the gold crayon, I drew a crown on top of his head.

The king from my dream was the safest dad I had ever met. I was pretty sure he was the man who sang the song over me in the woods. Seeing the two of us together in the forest near the little lake made my heart glad. In spite of the wolf lurking a few feet away, I felt safe.

As personal as my drawing was, I showed it to Beth. She went to great lengths to show it off, and she made sure that Katherine and Daisy took an interest. Daisy actually liked my picture and said it was perfect. Then Beth showed it to Adam Jr. and Susan. Adam Jr. had little to say. Susan said nothing at all.

That evening, Adam came home late from work and found the rest of us already eating dinner. He hung his jacket in the front hall, washed his hands, and sat at the table.

"How was your day, everybody?" he asked.

Beth answered first. "It was a gorgeous day, honey! How was yours?"

"I was stuck inside all day. That's the way it goes, I guess!"

It was a typical conversation for the Barnes's table but not one I'd grown used to yet. Then Adam turned to me, and my stomach flipped.

"What about you, Jessie?" he asked. "How was your day?"

"I drew a picture. It's on the fridge."

I was torn between enthusiasm and caution but hoped he would take an interest.

"You're kidding! Let's see it!"

He stood right up and went to the refrigerator. "Well look at that! You did a great job, sweetie!"

"Thanks," I answered sheepishly.

"Is that you?" he asked pointing to the drawing. "Are you the girl in the picture?"

"Yup."

"Oh. And there's a wolf. Or is that your dog?"

"No. It's a wolf that I've seen in real life."

Apparently feeling that the foster child was attracting too much attention, Susan joined the conversation. My earlier concern about being too transparent was about to be proven right.

"You've actually seen a real, actual wolf?" she sassed.

"I saw it in the woods when I...when Katherine and I ran away." I wondered why I bothered answering her.

"But there are no wolves in Texas, Jessie. You'll learn that when you get to the seventh grade. Wolves only live in cold or temperate climates."

"OK, Susan," Adam interrupted.

Adam studied my drawing for a few more seconds before returning to his dinner. I was relieved that he didn't ask any more questions about it, and I hoped that was the end of the matter. I suspected, however, that he saved some questions for later, when Susan was not around.

I was right. Before bed, I brushed my teeth while watching my reflection in the bathroom mirror. Suddenly Adam appeared behind me in the mirror image and stared at my reflection. I spun around to look directly at him.

With his usual smile and soothing approach, he said, "Jess, would you come talk with me for a minute?"

With my mouth full of toothpaste, I nodded.

"Good. I'll be in the living room when you're done."

I nodded again and Adam disappeared. Eager to hear what he had to say, I quickly rinsed my mouth and went to the living room, where he sat on the couch, alone. Everyone was getting ready for bed, so the living room was unusually empty and dark.

"Come sit here with me for a second," Adam said in hushed tones.

I sat a couple of cushions away and hugged a throw pillow to my chest.

"I wanted to ask you about the picture you drew."

With half a smile and a slight nod, I waited for what was next.

"Was that your dad behind you on the path? With the crown?"

"Yes." It didn't feel like I was lying.

"I thought so."

Adam paused and then continued speaking. "You did an amazing job on that picture, Jessie."

"Thanks."

"I can see that you really miss your dad. I'll bet you're sad about what's happening with your family, too."

Then my foster dad looked right into my eyes and said, "I'm sorry, Jess. I know it's tough."

I was taken with how much he cared about me and my feelings. No one but Mom had ever taken such an interest in how I felt. Yet I could not look at him. So I looked at the floor.

He asked softly, "Can you tell me why the wolf is there?"

"I don't know. I've seen him once in a dream and once in real life. He really is real, even if Susan says he's not."

I wondered why Adam wanted to know about the wolf. I didn't want to talk about it. I wanted Adam to ask

about my family and tell me again how good my drawing was.

"I did my best on my drawing. Beth said it's like a
work of art." I smiled, hoping Adam would agree and
praise my work. But he looked away.

After a long moment, he turned to me and said, "It's
very beautiful, Jessie. And you're very beautiful. Do you
know that? Do you know how proud I am of you?"

I felt my heart melt. Never had a man spoken so tenderly to me. Only the king in my dream had been as
kind. I could not stop smiling. Then Adam patted me on
the head and asked, "How about if you and I talk about
things from time to time?"

Lowering the volume of his voice some more, he said,
"We can meet right here, and you can tell me how you're
feeling. We'll discuss whatever is on your mind."

My broken heart leaped with fresh hope. "That
sounds really good."

"Wonderful! But this has to be our secret, OK?"

"OK," I whispered back.

"All right, kiddo. Now off to sleep."

I hopped up from the couch and floated to the bedroom, where Daisy and Katherine were already asleep. I
lay awake, glowing.

From that night on, my foster dad, Adam Barnes, regularly invited me into the dark, empty living room for our
secret talks. I was amazed that he stayed up for my sake,
even after everyone else had gone to bed. It meant the
world to me.

Once, when I talked about how mean Daddy was,
Adam put his arm around me, to comfort me. It felt so
good and fatherly and safe.

After awhile, Adam made it a habit to put his arm
around me each time we talked.

Later, he began saying that he loved me. He looked at
me the way Mr. Carter had.

One night Adam touched me and asked me to
touch him.

I didn't say no.

On another night in the dark, empty living room,
Adam took advantage of me completely.

I had just turned thirteen.

I wanted him to stop inviting me to the living room.
And yet, I didn't want him to stop.

I heard Daddy's words in my head. "Jessie is nothin'
to nobody. Nothin' but a worthless piece of meat."

When Daddy first said it, I could almost believe it was a
lie. I wanted to believe it was a lie, but Mr. Carter obviously
thought it was true. So did Adam. Now I believed it too.

Musical notes echoed in my mind...*G - A - B - G—*

Then I decided to forget them forever.

CHAPTER 12

→—·—←

TEN MONTHS AFTER running away, Katherine and I saw Mom and Daddy again. I wrapped my arms around Mom's neck and squeezed her with all my might. She pried herself away just long enough to look in my eyes. I don't know what she found there, but in hers I saw the depths of her pain.

Our reunion was necessarily brief. Mom gently tucked my hair behind my ear and squeezed me tight once more. We said little; there was no time for catching up and no appetite for discussing the reason for our reunion. We shed some tears, quietly smiled at one another, and dutifully let go.

I would have said hello to Daddy and might have hugged him. But that was not possible. He wore a white jumpsuit and sat at a sturdy table with his court-appointed lawyers. I tried to make eye contact, with no success.

Daddy kept his eyes lowered. Perhaps looking up would have been too much for him to bear.

Because I was the one who first planned to run away, I was the court's first witness. Sitting behind a wooden table and speaking into a microphone, I answered difficult and embarrassing questions. The stress made the experience surreal, as though my head had separated from my body and now floated above it. My anxiety raced through my right leg, which bounced incessantly as I dug into memories I longed to forget. I never sought to hurt Daddy; I only wanted to answer truthfully. I confess, however, that telling on him felt good.

The proceedings were difficult. The whole family suffered and many people in the courtroom cried. As I answered each question, I worried about the next one. Not knowing where to look, I often looked at Mom. More often than not, she stared at the floor. I realized that she was probably in the most agonizing position of all.

For four grueling days, all of my siblings except Ben testified. With Jake and Jason the lawyers focused on the beatings and on Daddy's fights with Mom. Katherine and Daisy answered questions about the hunting trips. Their testimony often drew gasps from the audience. None of it helped Daddy's cause. Many observers glared at him, and several jurors wept openly as my sisters described their ordeals.

I didn't cry with the jurors, but I mourned for my sisters. I understood their long silence more than I could have understood it before moving to Beaumont. Except for the single time I questioned Daisy, neither of the girls ever talked about their hunting trips with Daddy. I never told anyone what Adam did, either.

When all the testifying was finished, the judge asked the jury for their verdict. A woman juror stood up and said, "Guilty."

The judge sentenced Daddy to thirty months in the state prison at Clemens, Texas. The bailiff handcuffed him and led him out of the courtroom. I waited for him to look at me and maybe say something, but he never did.

That was the last time I saw my Daddy.

The judge ruled that the boys would continue to live at home with Mom, but my sisters and I would remain in foster care until we reached adulthood. Few foster homes could accommodate three children for the long term, so the judge ordered us girls to be separated. We would never again live under the same roof.

Once again, I knew there would be no turning back, no picking up where we left off. The situation was unbearable to the point of being mind-numbing. I felt disconnected even from myself, as though I were sleepwalking in a place I wanted to escape.

My family was permanently broken. The finality of separation was all too real. I looked around the room at each person I loved and whispered to them in my mind...

Good-bye, Jake.

Good-bye, Jason.

Good-bye, little Ben.

Good-bye Daisy.

Good-bye Katherine.

Good-bye, Mom.

As I tried to grasp what I was feeling, three child protection caseworkers appeared. Their job was to take me and my sisters to our respective foster homes. There was no chance to exchange final words with Mom or my brothers. And before I had a chance to say good-bye, Katherine was whisked away too.

I broke away from my caseworker, ran over to Daisy, kissed her forehead and said the only thing that came to mind. "It's OK, Daisy. It's OK."

Then Daisy was gone too. The Jenkins family was shattered forever. And it was my fault.

My caseworker and I traveled a long stretch of highway until a big city appeared.

Houston was a far cry from Woodcrest, but for the rest of my childhood, it was home. It was a good home too. The family that took me in gave me a safe place to live and my own room—two things I'd never known.

As typical as my new life seemed to be, on the inside I felt nothing in common with my friends and classmates. I was well cared for and went to school like they did. I learned to drive and got decent grades. But no matter how well I dressed or behaved, and no matter how hard I laughed, I could not escape the secrets I carried with me. I still felt like an uncivilized child from a wild kingdom surrounded by perfect people who were nothing like me.

How I wanted to be like my friends! How I longed to be carefree and innocent! The best I could do was play the part. I covered up the "real Jessie" with the right clothes, a good smile, plenty of makeup, and a practiced niceness. I was a fake.

As I grew up, I discovered that there was no possible escape from my past because what happened with Daddy, Adam, and Mr. Carter was no longer the issue that tormented me the most. Although I felt ashamed of what they did and even hated them for it, I hated myself more. My greatest fear in high school was that my friends would discover the Jessie I loathed—Jessie the whore—and would abandon me.

So I pretended to be someone else. Someone perfect. And happy. And normal.

My façade might have fooled others but not me. Within weeks of graduating high school, I thanked my foster family and said good-bye. They loved me and begged me to stay. They had done me nothing but good, so I knew their pleas were sincere. Yet I was determined to leave with only a duffle bag and a vague plan to go West.

I was barely an adult but already an expert at running away. I ran the night Daddy beat baby Ben. I fled Mr. Carter, and I ran away from home. Now I abandoned the perfect foster family, launching a years-long trek from one city and state to another. Every time I entangled myself with a guy or a job, I ran. When people got too close, I left before they could discover the Jessie I hated.

One of my escapes was to Las Cruces, New Mexico, where I held down a job but drank all day, every day. My boyfriend Antonio was a bouncer at a nightclub popular with college kids from Juarez. It was the perfect setup for a crash, and I crashed in spades.

At the club late one night, I danced alone in an alcohol- and pill-induced haze. My body was worn out, but the pounding bass inspired me to move. Some guy who was similarly inspired danced with me. I didn't know him and had never seen him before. I enjoyed dancing with him, until he touched my shoulders suggestively and kissed me.

Antonio must have seen the encounter. In no time flat the guy was stretched out on the floor and Antonio was dragging me into a back room. He slammed the door behind us, reminded me what a tramp I was, and proceeded to punish me for it.

I limped out of the club battered and hoping to die.

Alone at home the next day, the thought of dying consumed me. I drank a fifth of vodka, shouted obscenities at the walls, broke things, and devised a plan: I would visit Caballo Lake, stop for lunch, and enjoy the Southwest scenery. Then I'd watch the sunset, say a prayer, and drive my car off the dam.

The lake was an hour away and I was in no condition to drive around the corner. I got behind the wheel anyway. Halfway to the lake I stopped at a relic of a gas station, gave the counter attendant a five-dollar bill, and pumped my gas. When I got back in the car, I realized my keys were gone. I cussed my way back to the register and unloaded on the attendant.

"You stole my car keys!" I shouted, adding some choice expletives.

"Ma'am, I don't know what you're talking about. Why would I take your keys?"

"Because you think I've been drinking and you're gonna call the cops. That's why!"

He'd had his fill. "I didn't take your keys, lady. Now get outta here!"

I cussed my way back to my car and searched it more frantically. Reaching under the driver's seat for the umpteenth time, I found some unexpected comfort: a small bottle of vodka. I took a long slug and licked my lips. The next thing I remember, I was handcuffed to a hospital bed with the taste of vomit in my mouth.

After years of drowning bad memories with alcohol, the shock of jail time forced me out of denial and onto my long road to sobriety.

My next stop was Colorado, where I waited tables in a kitschy little eatery in Estes Park. The place was a much better fit than I ever expected. Colorado is a beautiful state with endless outdoor adventures. I often thought about how much Jake would have loved it. The high country was the perfect haven, and it was full of my best and oldest friends: tall, beautiful, predictable trees.

Often, after my daily shift, I would drive into Rocky Mountain National Park for a healthier kind of running. In the park I found the perfect place to be alone: a trail that started at beautiful (but touristy) Bear Lake and wound its way deep into the forest, past Emerald Lake where I could wander off-trail through the wilderness toward Flattop Mountain.

Early one afternoon after a tough shift at the restaurant, I ran especially hard. As I emerged from the forest, I paused at the edge of Emerald Lake. The shimmering water and granite peaks never failed to take my breath away. I continued my run, circling the water and making my way around the rocky terrain when, suddenly, the hair on my arms stood up and adrenaline surged through my gut. I stopped abruptly and scanned the area for the source of my alarm. I saw nothing, but I was sure I was not alone.

I was right. A dark shadow darted between the trees just inside the forest. The shadow paused for just a moment, then dashed out of sight.

It was no ordinary shadow. And it was no stranger.

CHAPTER 13

THE WOLF THAT FIRST stalked me in my childhood dream and later followed Katherine and me through the woods now hunted me again. My heart beat so violently, it was the only sound I heard—a thud, thud, thud pounding in my skull.

My legs begged to run. But where?

The wolf seemed to vanish into thin air, but my gut said it was lurking in one of ten thousand hiding places all around me. I suddenly longed to be at Bear Lake with all the tourists and their tacky t-shirts, but I'd have to go through the forest and its shadows to get there. My best option now was to stay in the clearing around Emerald Lake, where I could see the monster before it attacked.

If it did, the battle would be one on one, so I needed a weapon. Stones in every size and color surrounded the lake, but the ones I could get my fist around were too smooth for a good grip and too rounded to wound my stalker.

Finally, I spotted a jagged rock with the right size and shape to do some damage. I held it tightly and scanned the tree line for movement. I saw nothing.

Several minutes passed. Gradually, my heart stopped pounding and some semblance of peace returned. I knew I needed to head back to my car, whether the wolf was gone or not. The cooling mountain air signaled that night was only hours away, and I had some distance to cover.

Clutching the rock and scanning my surroundings, I ran toward the trail, even farther than seemed right but with no sight of it. I could not imagine having missed it, but I realized I must have done so.

Maybe my encounter with the wolf turned me around, I thought. So I followed the tree line back around the lake, knowing it would take me where the trail was supposed to be. When it didn't, I circled again.

How could I be lost when I know this place so well?

Renewed fear engulfed my heart. It seemed obvious—the wolf had to be some kind of supernatural being from who knows where. How else could it haunt my dreams and stalk me in real life? And why had it chased me all these years?

Does he have the power to move the trail? Am I trapped?

"What ifs" raced through my mind. I shook my head to clear it and reminded myself that I knew the area like I knew my own name. I walked the tree line again and—finally!—a trail appeared, on the wrong side of the lake. I'd never seen a second trail there and certainly not one leading away from Emerald Lake and deeper into the wilderness.

I was mystified but not quite panicked. Years of disruption had taught me to trust my instincts. I prided myself in not living like a lost little girl. Over time I learned that, one way or another, I could find my own way around this big, bad world. So I coached myself. *Follow your gut, Jessie. That's what got you away from Daddy. It will get you out of danger now.*

The confusion over the trail was baffling, yet I sensed somehow that I was precisely where I needed to be, and wherever this new path went, I would go. So I followed it away from the lake and upward into a beautiful stand of ponderosa pines. The landscape was unfamiliar but felt safe, like a newfound sanctuary. That wolf may have prevented me from returning to my car, but something lovely was leading me someplace new.

With every step, the world looked more alive. I studied bark patterns on tree trunks. I watched squirrels dropping pine cones from the treetops and scurrying down to bury them. I was awestruck at the deep blue of the cloudless sky and the crispness of the mountain air.

Finally, the new trail left the forest and brought me to a very small lake I'd never seen in my travels or on any map. I marveled at what a well-kept secret it was and how sweetly it sang to my soul. The air was perfumed with pine and earth. The sun's rays fell like a warm blanket on my cheeks. The place was perfection!

I knew I could not stay long, but I had to strip off my footwear and wade in. The ice-cold water felt so welcoming, as though I'd discovered a secret garden that existed only for me. Then I realized that the place wasn't so secret. Across the lake and near its edge, a youngish man sat on a boulder.

Years of encounters with devious men helped me develop a kind of radar that distinguished those who were safe from those who pretended to be. I could not explain how the screening worked or swear that it was foolproof. But I trusted it.

My trust wasn't naïve. I mentally catalogued every detail about the stranger. He wore blue jeans and a grey T-shirt. He had light brown hair under his camouflage cap. He held a fishing pole and dangled its line in the lake. He seemed equally aware of me and of the fact that he had startled me. Yet instead of avoiding eye contact, he looked straight at me, smiled, and waved.

He's safe, I thought.

Knowing someone else was there calmed any vestiges of fear but made me self-conscious. I watched as the man smiled again and raised his hand, not to say hello this time but to invite me to his side of the lake. I was torn between believing he was no threat and knowing by experience that invitations from men were threatening, period.

I chose to set aside my history and follow my gut. I walked toward the man and told myself, *You're going to be fine, Jessie. Everything is going to be OK.*

As I neared him, pain radiated from my fingertips and reminded me that I still clutched a rock. Approaching the stranger with a weapon would be awkward, but I wasn't particularly concerned about sending the wrong message. That rock was my insurance policy.

The man didn't seem concerned about it. He smiled warmly, as though we were already acquainted, and said, "Look at that!"

I turned to see the panorama behind me. Pine trees covered the nearest hillside and disappeared into a deep valley. Opposite the valley an aspen-covered slope displayed early fall colors. Behind the near hills loomed the backside of Long's Peak, its massive granite face dwarfing all else and obliterating the horizon. Treeless but exquisite, it was dotted with house-sized boulders and draped in bright white glaciers. Immovable as it was, its color changed continuously as sun and clouds coursed through the sky.

"Wow...that...is...amazing," I stammered.

"It is, isn't it?"

I smiled quizzically, thinking how odd it was to discuss the scenery before we knew each other's names.

He must have read my mind, because he stood to his feet and extended his hand. More unself-consciously than anyone I'd ever met, he said, "My name is Jason."

I smiled. "One of my brothers is named Jason. You know that means 'healer,' right?"

"Yes," he smiled back, with a hint of mischief. "I know."

"I—I'm Jessie." I shook his hand and turned aside shyly.

Jason's light brown hair poked out from under his cap, and a full, darker brown beard covered much of his face. He was good-looking, not in a way that attracted me to him but in a pleasant, safe sort of way.

"Did you find something there?" Jason asked, pointing to my rock.

"Oh yeah. Sorry." I giggled nervously and tossed the rock away. "Down at Emerald Lake I saw...well, I thought I saw a bear or a coyote or something."

I dared not mention the wolf. Seeing wolves where no wolves are known to exist had gotten me mocked once before.

Jason chuckled, but not with ridicule. "Better safe than sorry in the wilderness."

He casually resumed his fishing. Just as casually, I sat down beside him and asked whether he caught many fish in the tiny lake.

"Sometimes I do. Other times there don't seem to be any fish for miles."

"Ever catch cutthroat?"

"Yup," Jason answered. "Browns and brooks too."

I stood up and peered into the clear water, watching for movement. It was the best way to spot fish that blended with the colored rocks on the lake's bottom. Within seconds, something moved.

"Hey! There's something—right there!"

My "fish" was flat and rectangular.

"Oh, wait," I said, squinting my eyes and leaning over the water's edge. "It's a photograph!"

I waded ankle deep for a better look and followed the photo out of the sun's glare. What I saw took my breath away. It was a picture of a young girl playing outdoors with a toddler dressed only in a diaper. His chubby legs were covered with welts and fresh scabs.

In my head I screamed, *It's baby Ben!*

Suddenly other photographs floated up from the lake bottom and covered the water's surface. One showed Daisy sitting on a concrete step, hugging her knees. I sat next to her, doing the same. In another, Jake and I were in the woods at night, his face misshapen and caked in dried blood. Another photo showed Mom slumped over the kitchen table, bloody and looking dead. Other images showed Daddy with a switch in his hand. In one of them, I stood against the wall, my calves already beaten. Another picture showed Mr. Carter watching me play tetherball in the schoolyard.

My worst memories were documented in hundreds of images that surrounded me in the water. As they bumped against my legs, I stood speechless, gripped by a sense of betrayal, as though I'd been tricked into reliving the suffering I had so carefully packed away.

Then music filled my ears. *G - A - B - G - C - B - A...*

The notes penetrated the deep layers of pain that encased my heart. Yet they did not bring the peace they had brought me in the past.

I glared at Jason, who was humming behind me. "Who are you?"

Calmly, he said, "Jessie, I want to..."

"Who *are* you?"

He looked me in the eye, his own eyes brimming with the sadness I felt.

"You did this!" I screamed. "You wanted me to see these pictures. Why would you do this?"

Jason sat silently, making no attempt to defend himself or stifle my anger.

"And how do you know my song? I haven't heard it in years! Who are you?"

"Who do you think I am, Jessie?"

He spoke tenderly, not with the feigned tone of my foster father, Adam, but with a compassion that breached my inner walls.

I turned away from him and toward the pictures of my broken life. Then I ran.

"Jessie! Wait!" Jason pleaded.

As though deaf to him, I fled barefooted across the rocks, down the path, and back into the forest. I trembled as the images repopulated my mind. I had pushed them out of my head long ago and pretended the pain no longer existed. How expertly I convinced myself that I had moved on!

But the visions of abuse, hatred, and suffering now shattered my convictions.

The last thing I remember as I sped around a sharp turn on the path was my foot's excruciating collision with a protruding tree root followed by my full-body impact with the ground. The fall was significant enough that I would not remember it.

CHAPTER 14

THE USUALLY JOYFUL sounds of singing birds now made my head pound harder. Headache aside, I felt much too comfortable to be sprawled out on a mountain trail. I soon realized I was in my own bed, wearing my earth-stained clothes from the day before. My badly bruised knee and the lump on my head attested to a pretty good tumble. The fact that my knee was nicely cleaned up made me wonder.

A handwritten note stood folded on my nightstand, with my name inscribed on the outside. The message inside was straight to the point: "You took quite a fall, but you're going to be OK. We need to talk. Come back when you're ready."

The note was signed, "Jason."

I placed the note where I found it—beside two ibuprofen tablets and a glass of water, both of which I gulped down gratefully. With less than fifteen minutes to eat,

shower, and get to work, I decided that my injuries war-
ranted a sick day, whether I accepted Jason's invitation or
not. So I dialed the restaurant.

"Yeah," said Harry, the perfunctory morning cook.

"Hi, it's Jessie—"

"You aren't coming in, are you?"

"Well hello to you too, Harry."

I admit to playing up my sick voice, but I told Harry
the truth. "I have the worst headache of my life."

He couldn't resist. "Late night, eh?"

"Seriously, Harry. I feel like—"

"Yeah, yeah. I get it. The little lady needs to recuperate."

I wanted to reach through the phone and throttle
him. Then he added insult to injury with the most ado-
lescent question imaginable. "So...who's the guy?"

You have no idea, I thought.

The truth was that I had no idea. I blew off the question and said, "Look, I'll be in tomorrow. I just need to
rest today."

I hung up the phone and decided to visit Jason despite
the pain, the wolf, and the mystery surrounding the previous day's events. I knew it could be a bad idea. But my
life was already a mess, and I suspected that Jason was
part of it. I simply had to know more.

After some coffee and a shower, my headache van-
ished. I looked upward, thanked Jason for the ibuprofen,
and poured myself another cup. As I sipped, I reached

for the purple coin that had become a beacon in my life and read its inscription aloud: "Grant me the serenity to accept the things I cannot change, courage to change the things I can, and wisdom to know the difference. Amen."

I'd been sober for seven months since the episode in Las Cruces, but the prayer was still fresh. Eight months after my trip to rock bottom, I clutched my sobriety chip and hoped that another meeting with Jason would change something deep in my core. The fact that I hoped for *anything* was significant. Hopelessness had been my constant companion as far back as I could remember. During detox, I even doubted that God himself could change me. I was convinced that Daddy had been right about me. I was an unlovable, dirty piece of meat. All the bad choices I'd made since leaving my last foster home proved it.

Yet since meeting Jason, I had hope.

At the same time, I felt a certain fear about what was ahead. The wolf that stalked me since childhood had found me in the Rockies. The stranger at the lake knew my song and exposed me to my most anguished memories. I fell hard enough to lose consciousness and woke up in my bed with an invitation to return to the lake. Did I really want to risk all that again?

Meeting Jason again made no sense. But neither did the wolf or the effect of Jason's song all those years. And how on earth did my mother sing a song that she had never heard? How could she have known the melody?

None of these things added up. Yet they were very real. So I pressed harder on the gas pedal and made my way to the little lake. When I arrived Jason was fishing from the same perch, wearing the same outfit as he wore the day before. I quickly circled the lake to reach him and then spoke out boldly.

"Why did you do that?"

"What do you mean?" asked Jason.

I realized that even I had no clue what I meant. "OK, let me rephrase that. *Who are you?*"

"I'm your friend," he said gently. Reaching one hand behind his back, Jason lifted a piece of yellow construction paper off the ground and handed it to me. I recognized it immediately, though I hadn't seen it in over a decade.

"My drawing."

I studied it closely, shocked to be holding it in my hands again after so many years, and pleasantly surprised at what a good little artist I had been.

Suddenly I realized why Jason wanted me to see it again. "The forest...the lake...the wolf," I said, astonished. "And me...and...you?"

"Yes," Jason said softly. "You and I both have longed for this moment for a long time."

I sat down on a rock beside him and asked the next in a long line of questions that suddenly flooded my mind.

"So the song I heard when I was a kid—"

"I wrote it for you, Jessie. I wrote it *about* you." Jason reeled in his line and set down his rod. "I sang it to you when you hid in the log. After your bad dream, I sang it to you again, but this time I did it through your mom. Then I wrote the tune in your heart so you would always remember it."

"But why?" I shot back.

"Because I love you."

"This makes no sense whatsoever. How were you there? How did you find me here? Are you God, or something?"

Jason just smiled.

"Really! So where have you been since I ran away from home?"

"I've been with you! I was with you in the woods and everywhere else you went. I was at the kitchen table when your dad threw the bowl at your mom and when he broke Jake's nose. I was in the school attic with you and Mr. Carter. I know all about your siblings' suffering. I know what Katherine and Daisy have been through, and Jason and Ben too. I know about the insecurity Jake carries from your dad's hateful words. I've heard your mother cry more than you know. I've been there all along."

"I don't believe you. How could you watch it all happen? If you were there, you would have *done* something! Why didn't you stop Daddy? He was a monster! He ruined all of us! And you just watched and sang a song?"

Jason's eyes welled up as storehouses of anger poured out of my soul.

"Do you know how many times my foster dad raped me? Do you know that Jason is in jail? And Jake—I have no idea where he is! I do know that Katherine and Daisy are in bad shape. So am I. Eight months ago I planned to kill myself."

"I know, Jessie. I know. You didn't always see me, but I saw you every single day. I never left you...*never*."

"Why didn't you save us? *Why?*"

Tears soaked my face. "Daddy is dead! No one but Mom even went to his funeral. And, yes, I'm glad about that!"

I held nothing back, yet Jason never challenged my feelings or asked me to reconsider. He simply listened. When I was done, we sat on the boulder and wept together.

Then Jason stood up and said, "Come with me. I want to show you something."

He led me by the hand to the water's edge. I cringed at the thought of seeing the pictures again. He seemed to understand my repulsion. He tugged my hand and said, "It's OK, Jessie, I promise. Please look."

Resisting my fear, I looked. The pictures were gone. In their place was a dead fish, its mouth wide open and its fixed eye reflecting the sky.

"The world is broken, Jessie. Every person, every tree, every animal...none of it is the way I intended it to be."

Jason's words resonated somewhere deep inside where I recognized them as truth. "A shadow of death has corrupted everything, even your dad's heart. He was a broken man, Jessie, and broken people break things."

"That shadow..." I cut in.

"You've seen him. You've seen him in the forest. You saw him in your dream."

"The wolf."

"Yes, the wolf. His sole passion is to destroy. He wants to drag you into the shadow, Jessie. He has chased you since—"

"Since you gave me the song."

"Exactly."

"In my dream, he wanted to steal the pendant. But why?" I asked.

"The pendant represents the real you. And the song I sang to you in the woods—it describes the person I made you to be."

"Somehow, I knew that. But why don't you kill the wolf, or cage him, or do *something*? Can't you fix all this brokenness?" I asked motioning to the poor, dead fish.

Jason's eyes lit up.

"The process is already underway, Jessie. The day is coming—I promise you—when all darkness will be finished and all suffering will end."

He looked straight into my eyes.

"But not yet."

CHAPTER 15

JASON'S ANSWER WAS sufficient for the moment. Nothing seemed important except being with him. There was no need to talk. I was content to watch him and realize that he was the one who'd sung to me so long ago. I tried for years to imagine what he looked like. Sometimes I pictured him as the father-king in my dream. Physically, there was no resemblance, but Jason's presence affected me exactly as the king's presence had.

In our silence, my sense of being protected increased exponentially. That peace had eluded me for many years, so I wrestled with believing what Jason said—that he had not left me all that time. I had faced more horrifying and isolating events than I could count. At times I did sense a certain presence that convinced me I was not alone, but I still couldn't bring myself to fully believe that he had stuck with me through all the things I'd done.

Jason ended our silence with another invitation to the water's edge. "Come on, Jessie. It's time."

"For what?" I asked.

He said nothing. He simply extended his hand over the water, closed his eyes, and spoke under his breath in a strange language I'd heard before. Immediately, a stirring began, like some great force welling up from beneath the earth. Yet everything around us was still, including the wind.

The only sound I heard was Jason's voice. I held my breath and wondered what would happen next.

He continued speaking, and a roar began in the distance as though a train were approaching from across the mountains. The sound ripped through the peaks and grew stronger, rumbling like an avalanche and howling like a fierce wind that caused the trees to bend and shake violently under its power.

Despite the tumult, the lake's surface remained glassy and undisturbed. Then a strong, warm gust encircled us. It was so threatening that I grabbed Jason's arm. I wanted his protection, and I believed he would keep me safe.

Squinting in the wind, I peeked at him and saw perfect peace on his face.

The wind intensified now, disturbing the glassy lake and agitating it so powerfully that a massive spray filled the air. Soaked to the bone and feeling like a leaf about to blow away, I hung onto Jason for dear life.

Then the wind stopped and everything was quiet. I opened my eyes to find the lake divided down the middle by a perfectly dry pathway. Water was stacked high on either side of the divide, as though held in place by clear glass panels.

I stood in disbelief. "What is going on?"

"Take my hand," was all Jason said.

As he led me along that path, I saw what caused me to flee the day before. All the painful images that once floated on the surface of the water now hung like artwork on the vertical walls of water. My heart ached at the sight of them, but I no longer felt the need to run.

It was a welcome change! All my life I tried to forget the events and people who hurt me. I ran from every reminder of them because I believed that forgetting would allow me to move on. It never did.

Now seeing the awful images on display seemed right and good. Instead of dread, I felt a surprising calm.

"Jessie," Jason said, "it's important to remember the events of your life and acknowledge all that happened."

"Why is that?" I asked earnestly.

"Because your story is not what you believe it to be. You need to see it again. You need to understand what *really* happened."

The revelation was bittersweet. I was happy to learn that this remembering would be part of my healing. But I was painfully aware that my years of forgetting had postponed my wholeness. Now my days of running were finally over. I would choose to bravely face my past so I could embrace the beauty that was calling me forward.

Slowly but surely, I made my way through the gallery and allowed each image to enter my heart. Amazingly, all my forgetting had not erased my memories. It had only buried them under layers of pretense—the façades of happiness I used to create a phony version of myself.

Now, with my heart exposed and vulnerable once again, the past seemed even more painful. Never had I seen the Jessie in the pictures so clearly or hated her more intensely. I despised her childhood naïveté and whatever else caused adult men to take advantage of her. I hated the person she became. I hated her almost as much as I hated the men who hurt her or cared too little to help her.

More than anything, I hated the fact that *she* was *me*.

"Stop for a moment," Jason directed.

I obeyed and looked over to where Jason pointed at a picture of Katherine and me hiding in Ms. Wilson's bathtub.

"Who do you see?"

"Me. And Katherine," I answered plainly.

"Yes, that's right. Look at her, and at yourself." I looked deeply into the eyes of the scared little girl in the tub.

"That is Jessie," Jason continued. "And who is she?"

"A whore." Even I was surprised at how quickly that word came out of my mouth.

"Really?" Jason asked softly. "Look deeper."

I turned again to the photo and searched the eyes of the terrified little girl. Suddenly I felt transported, as though Katherine and I were physically in that tub again. I remembered exactly how I felt that day. I reconnected with the sadness, confusion, and every other emotion that overwhelmed my little heart.

"Was Jessie a whore then? Or was she a lovely little girl trying to deal with a reality she was not yet equipped to handle?"

I didn't answer.

"Did Jessie choose to be unloved by her father?"

"No."

A small crack opened in my self-hatred.

"Can we look at a few more pictures?" Jason asked tenderly.

"Yes. OK."

Jason took a few steps and pointed to another photo. I saw Mr. Carter handing me a bright red sucker in the hallway at school. The smile on his face induced the urge to vomit.

"Is that little girl guilty of a crime?" Jason asked assertively. "Did she deserve to be singled out and preyed upon?"

My eyes began to swell with tears. "I don't know. I don't think so. Maybe. I just don't know!"

"What makes you say that? Why don't you know?"

I paused before I replied. The words I was about to say had never previously escaped my lips.

"I hated him for deceiving me and for kissing me. It was repulsive and wrong. At the same time, it...felt nice. Not the kiss, but it felt nice to be *wanted*."

My words ended and sobs of shame ensued.

Jason took my hand, led me to the opposite wall of water, and pointed to another picture. "Like this?"

It was an image of Adam and me on the couch.

I wanted to shred it. Instead, I groaned under the weight of the emotions it conjured—emotions that had dictated my "good girl" façade for so many years. The scene reminded me of the unwinnable conflict between repulsion and shame on the one hand, and the strange, forbidden longing that drew me back to the living room every time Adam beckoned.

"I hate that picture," I managed to blurt out. "I hate that girl!"

"I didn't hate her." Jason's voice soothed my heart like a balm. "I never stopped loving her."

"But she did bad things!"

"Jessie," Jason's own voice shuddered with sorrow, "What happened to you was wrong. It was evil." He paused, as if trying to contain a dangerous emotion. "It infuriates me more than you know. All of this," he said with a sweeping gesture toward the other photographs, "happened *to* Jessie. It did not happen *because* of Jessie."

"But I kept going back to Adam."

"Precious Jessie," Jason pleaded, "a child can't possibly manage the flood of confused feelings you experienced. You longed for the affection of a father. That longing got twisted and was manipulated by broken men. It was never your fault."

Jason looked into my eyes and spoke words that began to heal my soul. "Everyone aches for the love of their Daddy."

I so wanted to believe everything Jason said about me. For the moment, I was happy just knowing that *he* believed it. There were too many years and layers of shame still plastered over my heart for the light to break all the way through. So I silently absorbed this new version of my story.

Then a question came to mind. "You said you were with me all along, right? So if you never left me, where were you?"

Jason took my hand, smiled, and led me farther along the path separating the walls of water.

He motioned to pictures as we walked. "I sang to you as you hid in the log. I cried for you through Mrs. Blevins' tears. I sang your song with you in the chicken coop and sang it again through your mother. I visited you in dreams. I comforted you through sweet Ms. Wilson. I protected you through the police officer who didn't take you home. I was your faithful companion through

Trixie. I met you each time you sat searching for the right notes at Adam and Beth's piano. I comforted you through strong trees and sang over you through tiny birds. I even stole your keys the day you wanted to drive off the dam. My dear, darling Jessie, I have never left you alone."

What Jason revealed overwhelmed everything that I had believed for so long. Now, as I examined each photo, I could somehow see the shadow of Jason's presence in them all. In fact, as I relived each memory, I could *feel* his presence.

When I had studied every last image, I exited the far end of the lake and sat on the first boulder I saw. When Jason joined me there, the lake waters closed up. The path and the pictures disappeared.

I was calm, but as I sat with my eyes closed, my mind returned to Woodcrest where I relived every storm that happened and revisited every person who caused me or my family pain.

"Jessie, you need to give them to me now."

"What do you mean?"

"Look at your hands."

My hands were balled into fists and tucked into my lap. The skin over my knuckles was taut and white.

"Give them to me," he said once more. "Adam, Mr. Carter, your father. The people who hurt you and those who neglected to save you. You're holding on to them as though you expect them to pay for what they did."

I opened my hands slowly, which released a new floodgate of emotions.

Jason continued. "They hurt you, Jessie. They cost you so much. But it's an impossible debt for them to repay. There is no sense dragging them and their lies around anymore. Give them to me. I have my own way to take care of the debt they owe."

Tears flowed in torrents, and I spoke in a way I'd never spoken before.

"Adam, you stole from me something that was not yours to take. You preyed on my pain. You hurt my body and hardened my heart. You made me believe that giving my body away was the only way I could be loved. I reject your lie! For years I wished you were dead. But you are not my problem anymore. You're Jason's. I forgive you."

My voice grew louder and stronger.

"Mr. Carter, I will not let you or the evil things you did hurt me ever again. Your deceitfulness convinced me that men are never safe. Now I know that's a lie. You don't deserve it, but I forgive you. You have no more power over my life!"

Light began bursting from my heart. Decrepit old weights lifted from my chest until my breath flowed freely. I continued addressing everyone who hurt me or looked away when they could have helped. I listed their offenses and summarized the debts they owed me. I took my time laying out my case and expressing the depths of my anger over the losses I suffered at their hands. Then I gave them to Jason.

Only one remained.

"Daddy, I don't know why you never found a place in your heart for me. I was your little girl. I needed you! I only wanted you to love me and believe in me. Every day I imagined how I would feel if you proudly sat me on your lap or carried me on your shoulders. But it never happened. I wanted to be more to you than a piece of meat. But that never happened, either. I'm not your whore, Daddy. I'm your daughter."

I took a deep breath to curb my sobbing so I could finish what I had to say.

"You were a monster, Daddy! You caused so much pain. But you're gone now and I refuse—*I refuse*—to drag you around with me one more day! I am finished with that. I am done being your victim! I forgive you, and I am letting you go."

By the time I finished, I had evicted twelve people from the space they occupied in my heart. Although I felt free, I wept bitterly. I soon realized that my tears acknowledged the losses I'd suffered. I was grieving just as I might grieve the death of a loved one.

Jason's eyes brimmed with tears.

"There is one more, Jessie."

"Who?" I asked.

Carefully enunciating each word, he said, *"Are you ready to believe that it's not your fault?"*

How much harder it was to forgive the one I hated most!

Intellectually, I understood that a little girl can't be blamed for the wanton acts of adults. Clearly, the mess into which I was born was *not* my fault. Yet a relentless voice accused me. It said that men treated me badly because something about me was dirty. It convicted me of being filthy and shameful because I allowed my foster father Adam to sleep with me.

Those vile accusations followed me all my life. A voice had whispered them in my ear over and over again. It convinced me that I was unloved because I was unlovable.

G - A - B - G - C - B - A...

Jason's voice swept over me like a wave of pure love and washed me in total acceptance. For the first time, I believed there could be a brand-new life ahead.

CHAPTER 16

IF FELT SO GOOD to free myself from the people I had dragged around with me since childhood. Yet something told me the whole crowd was huddled just outside my heart, waiting to be invited back in.

No thanks, I thought *That's over.*

As Jason dropped his line back in the water, I stretched my legs with a walk along the shoreline. Kicking pebbles in the sunshine, I remembered the fun Jake and I had throwing rocks back in Woodcrest.

For old time's sake, I skipped a nice one across the lake. "Yeah!" I said aloud. "Still got the touch."

Like a kid in a candy store, I gathered two handfuls of good rocks, set them down on the shore, and chose one rock to launch. Holding it just right, I leaned toward the level of the water, drew back my throwing arm, and—

"Oh no!" I cried in disbelief.

The floating pictures were back! Everyone I had already forgiven stared up at me from the surface of the water *again.* In utter frustration, I shouted at Jason, "I did what you said. I let them all go! Why are they back?"

Unruffled, Jason set down his pole and walked toward me.

"You did let go. But what happened, happened."

"What does that mean? Shouldn't it all be gone now? Why would I need to keep remembering?"

Those images are part of your story, Jessie. And that's a treasure, for you and for others."

"You call something as screwed up as my life *a treasure?*" I began to raise my voice. "I saw my mom being beaten more times than I can count. You saw that too, right? And you want to tell me that's a treasure?"

I turned to walk away.

"You don't see it yet, but your life gave you something valuable. You understand what it means to be broken. More than most people, you know how it feels to lose everything."

"So what?" I asked.

Jason spoke firmly. "I don't expect you to appreciate what happened or celebrate the pain you endured. I know I don't. But you can be happy about what's next."

He almost had me. Then he ruined it.

"There's much more ahead for you, Jessie, *and you're worth it.*"

Anger and shame raged inside me. "No, Jason. I'm obviously not worth it!"

Immediately, branches started snapping in the woods. Without thinking, I leapt backward. Then I saw why.

The wolf lunged and crouched low with a menacing growl. Not since my dream had I seen its sulfur eyes so clearly. Coiled like a spring, it prepared to pounce, its muscles twitching in anticipation.

"Jessie!" Jason shouted. "Look at me!"

I snapped my head around and looked straight into his eyes.

"You must believe me. You are incredibly valuable."

"That's not true!"

When I denied my value again, the wolf moved closer and bared its teeth.

"You are precious to me, Jessie! You are strong. You are kind—"

"No, Jason!" I interrupted. "You're wrong. I'm none of those things!"

The wolf growled louder as long strands of drool fell from its jowls.

"You are gentle, Jessie. You are brave and beautiful!"

"No!" I screamed. "I'm nothing but a damn piece of meat. No one but you will ever love me!"

With that, the wolf lunged. Its heavy paws pinned me to the ground, and its eyes released an acid glow. Its putrid breath was hot on my face. Its teeth were bared for the kill.

I closed my eyes and prepared to die.

Then Jason's voice rang out. "Get off her!"

Jason reached both arms around the beast and yanked it backward off my chest. Twisting around with great force, Jason hurled it into the forest, where it slammed through the brush and against the trees.

Amazingly, the wolf regained its footing and threatened again.

Jason cupped his hands around my face and asked, "Do you trust me?"

"Yes!"

"Then take my hands."

I did. The wolf's second strike was imminent, but Jason was tranquil and began to sing. *G – A – B – G – C – B – A...*

As the melody perfumed the air, the atmosphere shifted. The bloodthirsty wolf responded by pulling back its ears and lowering its head in submission.

Astounded and grateful, I closed my eyes and let the song wash over me. With every note, Jason poured out more of his love for me. It was impossible to hate myself while he sang my song. Even when he paused, the music resounded in my heart and through the forest. What I heard took my breath away. For the first time, I understood the song's words.

My beloved, my beloved, my Jessie is she,
perfectly loved, perfectly free.
The winter is gone, the darkness has passed.
My beloved and I are together at last.
My beloved, my beloved, my Jessie is she,
perfectly loved, perfectly free.
With kindness and strength, she brightens the earth,
with captivating grace and infinite worth.
My beloved, my beloved, my Jessie is she,
perfectly loved, perfectly free.
No shame or regret, not a blemish is found; in
my sweet Jessie's heart only beauty abounds.
My beloved, my beloved, my Jessie is she,
perfectly loved, perfectly free.
Come away, come away, come away with me my dear.
My beloved, dear Jessie, come and dance without fear.

As Jason sang, an inexplicable light engulfed me. Its radiance was so intense that I shielded my eyes and was no longer sure of where I was. All I saw was a brilliant light surrounding me. Then, within seconds, it faded and the lake was visible again.

I did not immediately realize what happened in the light. But as my eyes adjusted and I looked down, I saw that my garments were changed, and great jewels adorned me. Diamond bracelets wrapped my wrist and diamonds hung from my neck. My attire was grand—even royal. The skirt portion of my purple-and-white gown flowed from a high waist to the tops of my bare feet. Its short sleeves were arranged to look like the petals of a delicate flower.

Never had I felt so beautiful!

Like a prince wooing his princess, Jason took my hand and sang once more:

Come away, come away, come away with me my dear.
My beloved, dear Jessie, come and dance without fear.

As he guided me toward the water, I leaned stubbornly in the opposite direction.

"Do you still trust me?" Jason asked.

"Yes, but I am afraid."

"I understand," he said.

Jason continued walking backward and leading me into the water. Then, without a hint of hesitation, he stepped onto the surface of the lake! Ever so gently, he tugged my hands and invited me to do the same.

"Come with me, Jessie. Come with me on the water."

I could not imagine how, but I stepped onto the water and danced with Jason on its glassy surface! It was magnificent, not only because we defied nature but because of what I saw in Jason's eyes. It was the look I longed to see in Daddy's eyes—the assurance that I was safe with the one who loved me.

Overwhelmed and showing my lack of experience with such goodness, I danced more awkwardly than I thought possible, crushing Jason's toes again and again. Instead of scolding and shaming me, he said, "I'm so proud of you, Jessie. I'm so very proud."

My face turned scarlet. I lowered my eyes and saw the pictures in the water beneath us.

"Now Jessie," said Jason, "let's not forget the past. Let's dance on top of it."

As he sang my song, we waltzed and twirled and swayed across the lake for an hour or more. How I wished our dance would never end!

But it did, and Jason led me back to the shore.

I felt no sorrow or disappointment but only contentment. I spread my arms wide in the pink and yellow sunset and inhaled the cool of evening. Never had I felt more alive and serene than in that moment. And never had I been so grateful.

"Thank you, Jason. I feel so beautiful, like…"

I was too bashful to continue.

"Like what?" Jason asked with a knowing smile.

"Like a princess. You make me feel so special and so loved. If only I could always feel this way."

"You can, Jessie. I didn't change you. I revealed the person you have always been. This," he said with a princely gesture, "is how you always look to me."

Jason smiled and turned toward the boulder where he'd left his things. As we walked there together, an incongruous buzzing sound invaded our space. It was my phone, vibrating on the boulder where I'd left it.

The caller ID unleashed legions of butterflies in my stomach.

"Kat? Is that you?"

"Hey, Jess."

I hadn't heard her voice in years, so I knew she wasn't calling just to chat. I avoided any small talk and cut to the chase.

"How are you, Kat? Is everything OK?"

Her voice withered. "Mom is sick, Jess. She's dying."

CHAPTER 17

THE DAY AFTER Katherine's call I flew into Houston, where the air felt hotter and stickier than I remembered it being. It was good to see Katherine again, but it was also painful. A lot had happened since the judge separated me and my sisters. Yet Katherine and I said little during the two-hour drive from the airport to Woodcrest.

Woodcrest had barely changed. Ladybird Johnson Elementary had not changed at all. A couple of new homes and businesses did little to upset the sameness. I took no comfort in that. Even the familiarity of my childhood home disappointed me as we turned into its long driveway. I squeezed the grab handle above my head and tried to ignore the churning in the pit of my stomach.

The little house was in a rough state. The exterior paint was faded and scratched. Some of the siding was loose, and some boards were rotted and hanging cock-eyed. Nostalgia and the smell of mildew overcame me as I stepped through the front door and into the dimly lit living room. The old brown carpet was terribly worn. The kitchen table was clear. The wall where little Ben took his first beating looked beaten itself.

The sight of Mom affirmed the passage of years. She was wrinkled and diminutive, virtually swallowed by her stuffed chair. Plastic tubes that provided oxygen and pain relief dangled awkwardly from her body. Her gaze seemed fixed, as though she was unaware of what was happening around her.

"Mom, someone is here to see you!" Katherine said with practiced cheerfulness.

"What Kath...?" Mom's raspy voice trailed off.

"Look who came to see you!"

Mom's eyes opened wide and her smile beamed with recognition.

"Jessie!" she said, struggling to stand and hugging me more powerfully than seemed possible for a woman in her condition.

I choked back tears and said, "Hi Mom."

She allowed her own tears to flow freely.

"My precious Jessie! My beautiful girl! You're home!"

It was wonderful to be in Mom's presence after so many years! How good it felt to hug her close and hold her soft hands in mine. Despite her sudden vigor, I knew she was weak. I urged her to sit down and drew up a chair so I could sit close by.

Mom and I talked about the house and the town. She tirelessly brought me up to date on the lives of everyone I knew from childhood.

"Old Rowdy will be happy to see you, Jessie."

"He's still alive?"

"Barely."

"Who takes care of him?"

"Jake and his girlfriend live up in Clarksdale. Jake comes down most days to look after the poor old fella."

Hearing that Jake was all grown up with a life of his own made me smile. And to think that after all these years, he still looked after that rascal stallion!

That's Jake, I thought. *That's just like him.*

"Mom, I'll be back in a minute. I've got to see Rowdy."

Stepping through the side door, I was surprised by everything that once looked so impressive and large. The pit that Jake and I dug survived, but it was full of half-burned trash.

I was strong back then, I thought to myself.

The outdoor wonderland and the barn we played in seemed small to my adult eyes. As I imagined the forts we made from hay bales and the sounds we made in our make-believe wars, I realized how tiny our pretend world was. One by one, the memories helped me reconnect with Jessie, the little girl, and showed me how much I liked the brilliant and adventurous person she was.

Even Rowdy looked smaller, but I enjoyed stroking him and looking into his big, black eyes. He wasn't the sturdy stallion I remembered, but he was as outgoing as ever. Whether he remembered me or not, I can't say, but he certainly enjoyed the attention.

My visit with Rowdy was short. Katherine had already warned me that Mom could pass at any moment, and the last thing I wanted to do was squander precious time. When I walked back inside, Mom greeted me with her sweet smile, as though she, too, wanted to savor every remaining moment.

I took my seat beside her, tucked her silver hair behind her ear, and stroked her hands, wishing I could buy time somehow. Katherine excused herself to go pick up some groceries. I was sure she did it purposely to give Mom and me some time alone. I had no idea how long she'd been caring for Mom, but I was touched by the fact that after all these years, Katherine still loved caring for others.

My earlier conversation with Mom seemed to have caught up with her, so we sat in silence for stretches of time. In the quiet, a stream of good memories, including some that had not surfaced since I left home, crossed my mind. I remembered certain adventures with Jake, and how much I loved tetherball. I remembered Trixie, our German Shepherd, and how brave she was against the rattlesnake. I laughed about the fits of giggles my sisters and I had at bedtime and thought about how Mom hid her own giggles when she ordered us to go to sleep.

Remembering these things helped me to see that not everything about our lives in Woodcrest was awful. In the midst of it all, we loved one another.

Then Mom broke the silence and broke into my heart.

"I love you, Jessie Ann."

"Oh, Mom, I love you, too!"

"You have always been so brave—even more than the boys, although I would never tell them that."

She giggled and cleared her throat.

"There were things I never told you when you were little, Jessie—good things that I should have said. Back then we thought that if you said a lot of nice things to your children, you would ruin them. I know now that it wasn't true."

I sensed that Mom was preparing to share something she had wanted to say for a very long time.

"I'm not the only one who loved you, Jessie. Daddy loved you too. Did you know that?"

I shook my head.

"Do you believe it now?"

I turned away and shuddered, tears pouring down my cheeks.

"He knew you, just like I know you. You are a good girl, Jessie. You're kind, and willing to work hard. You did more around this house than any of the other kids. And I should have told you more often how beautiful you are. I wanted to say it every day. I wanted to, but I didn't."

Mom's voice cracked under the weight of her regret. "You are precious, Jessie. You're precious to me. And you were precious to Daddy. He was a broken man. We know it, and he knew it. But I made mistakes too. Neither of us got it right."

"Mom, why didn't you stop him? He hurt us so much."

Mom cracked and began to wail, as though the dam restraining her emotions suddenly ruptured.

"I'm so sorry, Jessie. You'll never know how sorry I am."

At a loss to console her, I wiped her cheeks with a tissue.

"I thought about running away with you kids so many times. Daddy said if I did, he'd kill me. I told him I didn't care. Death would be easier than any life I could have with him."

I kissed Mom's sweet, wet face.

"There was only one reason I didn't go. I was afraid that, if he killed me and got away with it, you kids would end up alone with him. That scared me more than anything. So I stayed."

My heart nearly burst. Mom's explanation laid so many questions to rest. For years I blamed her for not rescuing us from Daddy. I had no clue about the choices she faced. All those years, I judged her based on my suffering. I never stopped to think about her sacrifice.

I rose out of my seat and squeezed into Mom's chair. Then I wrapped myself around her and whispered in her ear.

"I love you, Mom. I don't blame you for what happened. And I think I'm OK now."

She cried some more and then drifted off to sleep.

It had already been a long day, and I was sleepy too. As the sound of the steady rainfall filled my ears, I drifted off to sleep in the chair with Mom.

As we slept, I experienced the most fantastic dream of Mom and me flying and laughing euphorically as we did. At first we soared over Woodcrest. But soon we looked down on the tall pines and rugged cliffs of Colorado. When our feet touched the ground at the little lake I had recently discovered, I searched the shoreline for Jason, who was sitting in his usual spot with his line in the water.

Suddenly, my character seemed to recede, as if I was no longer a participant but an audience member watching the scene unfold. Jason reeled in his line, then stood up and walked toward my mother. Mom walked briskly in his direction, as though she knew who Jason was. Then they embraced like dear friends.

At this point the dream had no sound. But there was no mistaking what happened next. Mom held Jason's hands in hers and looked deeply into his eyes. Then she relaxed and closed her own. Her face seemed to melt into a peaceful expression like none I had ever seen on her. Though I could not hear, I could tell that Jason was singing.

I awoke hours later, when Katherine's hand touched my shoulder.

"Thanks for waking me up. I didn't mean to sleep so long."

"Jessie."

My heart seemed to stop.

"No!" I said loudly, turning toward the slouched, lifeless body beside me in the chair.

I was furious with myself for having fallen asleep. Frantic with grief, I knelt in front of Mom and kissed her cold hands. I curled her hair behind her ears and stroked her cheek. How I wished she would come back, even for a moment! How I longed to say good-bye!

"I love you, Mom," I sobbed. "I'm so sorry. I'm so sorry for everything!"

There was so much more to say and no possibility of saying it. There had been no proper good-bye when I ran away, and there would be none now. There could be no second chance. My mistake could not be undone.

I felt myself drowning in my emotions. It was a familiar feeling—too familiar. So I did what always came next: I ran, past the chicken coop, past the barn, and beyond our property line, far into the trees.

Yet this time was different. I fled to my forest sanctuary but chose not to run from my feelings. I examined my melding thoughts of grief and regret and worked to untangle them. I realized that although Daddy's death had broken my heart, it did not compare to the unbearable loss I now felt. Mom was my anchor. No matter how far I ran from the past and from Woodcrest, I always knew where she was. Now she was gone, and I felt like a toy boat adrift in the ocean.

Less than twenty-four hours ago, I had walked on water. I thought about my time with Jason and especially about our dance. The experience was still real. I increasingly believed everything he told me and everything I learned about who I was. But nothing would change the fact that my mother died. I knew that if I let it, her death would define my life the way other tragedies had in the past.

As I walked through the trees waves of doubt rolled over me. I wondered whether I was still under the curse of brokenness that had perpetuated my suffering for so long.

Maybe it's time to run again.

Maybe it's time to end it all. Why wait for another terrible thing to happen?

Once we bury Mom, I can disappear forever.

These familiar thoughts were strangely comforting. Yet deep down I no longer believed that running away

was my only choice. I recognized what I had never con-
sciously acknowledged before: I could run now and deal
with my pain later, or I could acknowledge my anguish
head-on and allow myself to heal.

"Jason!" I screamed. "This hurts so bad."

I couldn't see him, but I knew he heard me. So I
poured out my heart. "Why? What else can I lose? My
childhood and my innocence were stolen. My brothers
and sisters are scattered. Now Mom is dead! What more
do you want from me?"

I was angry, but I understood how much I needed
Jason and how desperately I wanted him to show up.

"What am I supposed to do now, Jason? Tell me, and
I'll do it!"

I closed my eyes and waited. Nothing happened, so I
turned and left.

On my way back to the house, I spotted something
jutting out of the thick brush. It was the abandoned
pickup truck Katherine and I found as children! I kicked
through the sage and inspected the rusty relic. The wind-
shield and windows were still intact. The black leather
bench seat was in good shape. The cardboard box was
exactly where I had left it the morning we ran away.

The door opened easily, releasing the stuffy smell of
the truck's cab. I pulled the box toward me and smiled
when I saw Katherine's Barbie doll and two desic-
cated peaches sitting on top of our folded clothes. I dug

deeper and found the photos Katherine had gathered before we ran away. I remembered wanting to study them at the time but deciding that we would run first and reminisce later.

Later had finally come.

On top of the stack was a picture of Daisy and Katherine in front of the barn with Daddy and Rowdy. Beneath it was a photo of some cousins I barely knew. There were several pictures of my brothers and sisters, old family friends, relatives, and some other people I barely remembered. But there wasn't a single photo of me.

I wondered, *Why didn't Katherine cut out any pictures of me?*

A voice deep within me nudged, "Take a closer look."

I examined every face in every photo. In each case, I saw at least one person whose eyes reflected the brokenness that only broken people recognize. The look tore at my heart. It was the same look I'd seen in the mirror countless times and in my loved ones' eyes as far back as I could remember. What shocked me was that my cousins had it too, although I had never noticed it till now.

Suddenly the secret Mom shared with me became even more meaningful. I realized that everyone is wounded, some more gravely than others. Every human being has been hurt by another human being, and everyone has secrets. For some, the wounding seemed inconsequential at the time but caused a lingering self-doubt, distrust, or insecurity. For others, the wrong was so damaging that they loath themselves for it, as I had done for years.

Everyone can find evidence of their pain in a family album. I had already found mine. The "missing" photographs from Kat's pile—the ones that reflected my own brokenness—were at the lake. I had already seen them. Jason used them to rewrite the story of my past and transform my future. In each memory, I had discovered Jason's presence, like a flicker of his love shining through the kindness of people and even the beauty of nature. I also found an innocent little girl who was preyed upon by broken men. She wasn't dirty, and she wasn't meat.

My personal suffering no longer needed validation. My memories were real enough. I could revisit them whenever I chose, not to rehash the horrors but to change the future—not only for myself but for others.

It's just as Jason said. My story is a treasure—for me and for them. He had comforted me through others. Maybe he would comfort others through me.

I dropped the pictures into the carton and left it all in the pickup. Then I looked for something hidden deeper in the woods—and found it! It was the hollowed-out, partially buried log with bark that looked like puzzle pieces all glued together.

This is where my healing began. It started all the way back then!

I sat on the log and ran my hands across the bark, not picking off the loose pieces and tossing them away but leaving them in their beautiful imperfection. The now familiar sense of peace swelled in my heart, and I realized that I was not alone. Jason had answered me in an unexpected way. He didn't take away my pain. He showed me how to dance on top of it.

I smiled and sang my song aloud, for the first time believing every word of it.

With kindness and strength, she brightens the earth,
with captivating grace and infinite worth.
No shame or regret, not a blemish is found; in
my Jessie's heart only beauty abounds.

Another voice, rising from somewhere out in the trees, continued:

My beloved, my beloved, my Jessie, is she;
perfectly loved, perfectly free.

My song is true. I am the Jessie God created me to be—perfectly loved and perfectly free.

DEAR READER

IN 2016, JEREMY and I sensed that God had a message to share through us. It turns out this message was for you!

Jessie's Song is a kind of parable inspired by the life experiences of someone I love very much—Jeremy's mom. No two stories are alike, but everyone has a story, and everyone has wounds. If you have experienced abuse, much of your suffering may have been done in secret. Classmates, coworkers, friends, and even your spouse might be unaware of your story and of the burden you carry.

My hope is that Jessie's story speaks to you and awakens a sense of your inherent value as a person. That is your true identity! You are not an accident or a mistake of nature. You were created by God in love and your worth is immeasurable.

If you feel forgotten or hopeless or lost, I pray that Jessie's encounter with Jason will remind you that you are not alone. There is One who came as a man yet is truly divine. He never forgets people or debases them but only restores and heals. His name is Jesus, and he knows every pain you carry in your heart. Even if you have never shared your story with a living soul, and even if you have chosen to forget, he remembers.

Jessie had a song. You do too! If you will ask Jesus, he will give you new life. He can teach you to dance upon your past as the infinitely valuable person you were born to be. He hears your cries and longs to answer them, regardless of how wounded you might be or how hopeless you might feel.

For more information and to find your next step, I invite you to join the conversation with Jeremy and I at the sites listed below. I hope you will invite others to visit too.

With love,
Rachel Williamson

jessiessong.com
Facebook: fb.me/jessiessongbook

SEASONS OF MY LIFE

A Poem by Arlene Alexander

God created a little girl who was born one day
to a mom and dad who were there to stay.

Such love and laughter, such joy and fun,
from early morning till setting sun.

Brothers and sisters together every day,
not a care in the world just adventure and play.

As seasons changed and years passed by,
it was time for school; it was time to cry.

Such callous teachers and principal too.
welts on her legs — everyone knew.

A season of sorrow, anger, and shame.
Did no one care? Did she cry in vain?

Things were said by a dad she thought she knew.
Bewildered and frightened, they just couldn't be true.

He spoke words which pierced her heart like a knife.
They would stay with her for most of her life.

Her hopes and dreams were shattered that night.
Would there always be darkness? Could she ever find light?

On tear-stained pillow, crying out in the dark,
the things he said had left their mark.

Nowhere to go, but she had to get free.
She escaped to the woods, to her puzzle tree.

So peaceful and quiet as the light broke through.
The rays of the sun so pure and true.

Gone were the days of the loved ones she knew.
To be replaced by someone new.

Time went by with a new family.
But soon things were not what they were meant to be.

Gone was the trust and security.
Replaced by confusion and impurity.

Storm clouds gathered and rain would fall.
Whispers blew through the trees; she heard them all.

Will there be no end to this pain and sorrow?
Will there ever be a better tomorrow?

Another home. Another family.
With care and happiness given freely.

A place to rest. A place to heal.
A place with love that she could feel.

Years went by with a family of her own.
Much more love than she had ever known.

Yet secrets of her past reared their ugly head,
filling her heart with fear and dread.

She tries to run to get away
from all the pain that wants to stay.

She goes to church. She learns to pray.
In this new house she wants to stay.

Songs of love and praise so free.
So much hope, how can this be?

Seasons come and seasons go.
Life goes on, but this she knows.

Mercy and grace, forgiveness too,
come from Him, and that is true.

Pain and sorrow grow very dim
as she opens her heart and stays close to Him.

She knows where to go and how to be free.
She runs to the woods and to her tree.

There He will be with arms open wide.
As the light breaks through, He's by her side.

The rays of the Son are so pure and true.
He's always there for me and you.